FORBIDDEN WITH THE DUKE

BY
ANNIE CLAYDON

TEMPTED BY
DR OFF-LIMITS

BY
CHARLOTTE HAWKES

MILLS
BOON

Cursed with a poor sense of direction and a propensity to read, **Annie Claydon** spent much of her childhood lost in books. A degree in English Literature followed by a career in computing didn't lead directly to her perfect job—writing romance for Mills & Boon—but she has no regrets in taking the scenic route. She lives in London: a city where getting lost can be a joy.

Born and raised on the Wirral Peninsula, in England, **Charlotte Hawkes** is mum to two intrepid boys who love her to play building block games with them and who object loudly to the amount of time she spends on the computer. When she isn't writing—or building with blocks—she is company director for a small Anglo/French construction company. Charlotte loves to hear from readers, and you can contact her at her website: charlottehawkes.com.

Published in Great Britain 2017
By Mills & Boon, an imprint of HarperCollins*Publishers*
1 London Bridge Street, London, SE1 9GF

© 2017 Annie Claydon

ISBN: 978-0-263-93330-7

FORBIDDEN NIGHT WITH THE DUKE

BY
ANNIE CLAYDON

ur policy is to use papers that are natural, renewable and recycl...
products and made from wood grown in sustainable forests. The ...
and manufacturing processes conform to the legal environme...
regulations of the country of origin.

Printed and bound in Spain
by CPI, Barcelona

Dear Reader,

I'm one of those people who sometimes finds it hard to keep a secret. The days before birthdays and Christmas are full of agonising anticipation for me—will my family and friends like the surprises I've carefully planned and have in store for them?

But of course there are so many kinds of secrets. And knowing exactly when to keep a secret is an art. No one expects that a confidence shared with someone we trust will be betrayed. And there are some things that don't need to be said and will only cause others unnecessary pain. But there are some secrets that will eat away at us and poison our world.

Megan Wheeler and Jaye Perera both have their secrets. But the challenges they face bring them to the realisation that the things they *don't* say have much more of an effect on their lives than the things they do.

Jaye and Megan took me with them on a fascinating journey from the splendours of an English country house to the magic of Sri Lanka. I hope you enjoy reading their story as much as I did writing it.

I'm always thrilled to hear from readers, and you can contact me via my website, at annieclaydon.com.

Annie x

To all those who run to help.

Books by Annie Claydon

Mills & Boon Medical Romance

Stranded in His Arms

Rescued by Dr Rafe
Saved by the Single Dad

The Doctor She'd Never Forget
Discovering Dr Riley
The Doctor's Diamond Proposal
English Rose for the Sicilian Doc
Saving Baby Amy

Visit the Author Profile page
at millsandboon.co.uk for more titles.

**Praise for
Annie Claydon**

'This is such a beautiful story filled with lots of
emotion as two people get a second chance at love,
and one that is so well deserved.'

—*Goodreads* on
Rescued by Dr Rafe

CHAPTER ONE

IN THE SCHEME of things it wasn't so much of a catastrophe. The building was still in one piece, no one had died, and the sun was still shining outside. But as everyday disasters went, this one was about the worst that Megan Wheeler could imagine. She'd really wanted this job, and now it seemed an impossibility.

It had all been going so well. The interviews had been tough but constructive, and her confidence had been vindicated when a job offer had arrived in the post. There would be a four-day induction workshop in Gloucestershire, hosted by the charity she would be working for, which would be attended by delegates from a number of different charities.

She'd packed her suitcase carefully, allowing for an outfit to meet every eventuality, and an early start meant that she'd been able to make the drive to Holte Hall in good time, stopping off for a cup of tea to make sure that she didn't arrive embarrassingly early, or mortifyingly late.

Excitement thrilled through her as she followed the signs which led from the elaborate gates up to the hall. The massive house rose on the horizon, all ornate stonework and grand windows, and as she drove towards the group of cars in the curving driveway, two teenaged boys waved her into a parking space and then directed her towards the impressive, canopied entrance.

John Ferris, the chief executive of the charity she was to work for, was standing in the cavernous hallway, ready to greet everyone. He expressed his pleasure at seeing her again, and passed her over to another teenager, who showed her to her room.

There was scarcely time to appreciate the elegant bedroom, with its modern, gleaming en suite bathroom, before she was summoned back downstairs again. Twenty or so people were chatting over coffee and pastries, and by the time the group was ushered towards the chairs that were set out at the far end of the room, Megan had exchanged nervous smiles with a number of her fellow delegates.

John Ferris had stood up to say a few words. All of the four different charities represented here would be holding sessions designed to equip the new recruits for the jobs that awaited them. He'd leave it to their host, the owner of Holte Hall, and chairman of the board of trustees of his own charity, to give them an idea of what the next four days had in store.

He gave a grinning shrug, running his hand across the bald patch on the top of his head. 'When we can find him, that is…'

It was clearly not unusual for their opening speaker to go missing. Someone opened the door a couple of inches and called along the hallway, and a thrill of nervous laughter ran around the room. Then the bottom of Megan's world suddenly dropped out, leaving her suspended in a mixture of horror and disbelief.

Jaye Perera.

Jaye had always known how to make an entrance, and this time it was no different. Fairy-tale handsome, with long-lashed brown eyes, which gave a touch of softness to an otherwise wholly masculine face. Dark hair that curled around the collar of his open-necked shirt. It was as if he'd been designed with the express purpose of making the female heart beat a little faster.

His dress and demeanour implied approachability, but his immaculate grooming indicated that he could be as smart as the next man if he put his mind to it. Megan heard the young woman sitting next to her catch her breath.

Most people did that. When she'd first seen him five years ago, sweeping through the hospital ward, deep in conversation with one of the senior doctors, Megan had done it. The dark good looks of his Sri Lankan father, along with the title he'd inherited from his mother's family, tended to make an impression. And when Jaye apologised for not being where he was supposed to be at the appointed time, his regret seemed heartfelt.

But Jaye Perera had a history of not being where he was supposed to be. He hadn't even turned up at his own wedding.

'Welcome, everyone.' His smile swept the room, and even Megan couldn't help the involuntary response, feeling herself smile back at him. 'This is a new venture for us. We've got together with three other charities to provide this induction course for doctors and nurses wishing to work abroad. We have session leaders here from each of the four charities, who'll be sharing their experience and giving you a taste of the realities of what you've signed up for.'

He was a good speaker, Megan had to give him that. In just a few moments he'd got his willing audience in the palm of his hand, everyone believing that he was speaking to them alone.

'Working abroad for a charity is something that many medical professionals aspire to, but the truth of it can be a little different from the theory. You'll be faced with hard work, challenging conditions, frustration and more than a little heartbreak. It won't matter that the pay's not what you could hope to earn in other fields, because you probably won't get much of a chance to spend it.'

A ripple of laughter flowed around the room. If Jaye was trying to change anyone's mind, he wasn't making much of a start. But then he knew that. This was all a PR manoeuvre, a deftly arranged exercise in making everyone think that he knew what working abroad was really like. Megan doubted he'd ever really got his hands dirty.

'Okay. So who has a significant other…?' His gaze ran around the room, seeming to pause for a moment on Megan, who was one of the few who hadn't raised her hand.

Jaye nodded. 'Well it's not rocket science to say that working abroad does affect family relationships, and we're interested in your thoughts about how you're going to deal with that…'

Megan felt herself flush. Jaye Perera had the out and out gall to talk about other people's relationships? When he'd walked out on his pregnant fiancée three days before their wedding?

She could hardly hear what Jaye was saying through a blur of misery. She'd really wanted this job, but working for a man like him? Being expected to follow his lead, when she knew that he had no sense of integrity? It was impossible, and she had to let it go now.

She sat through Jaye's talk, feeling her dreams slip away. There was going to be a buffet lunch at one o'clock, which was obviously intended to be a chance for everyone to start getting to know each other, and that would be Megan's chance to leave inconspicuously.

Easier said than done. When everyone rose from their seats, the knot of people surrounding her kept her waiting for a way out of the room. Jaye, on the other hand, had clearly acquired the knack of making his way through the obstacle course of empty chairs and groups of people who were intent only on talking, his way opening up before him in response to his dazzling smile.

'Lord Marlowe.' Megan might not be able to run, but she could hide behind the formality of his title.

'Nurse Wheeler.' He somehow made it sound as if he thought her title actually meant something, more than his maybe. That was a sham, too. On the occasions that he'd come into contact with her at work, he'd seemed only to see and hear the senior staff, as if the other people busying themselves around him didn't exist.

'I'm surprised you remember me.' The paper badge on the lapel of her jacket gave only her first name. The *nurse* part might be a lucky guess, but *Wheeler* couldn't possibly be.

'It's not difficult to notice someone who does her job well.' The comment was clearly designed as a compliment, but Megan knew it had no substance. Maybe he'd just studied the applications carefully and had a good memory.

'As you've already spent some time working abroad, we're hoping you'll be able to share some of your experience with the others,' Jaye continued smoothly, as if he already knew what *he* wanted to say, and her replies didn't make much difference to him.

She could play along, and then disappear quietly. Or she could show him that *she* had a good memory, too.

'How's Sonia? We didn't hear from her after she left the hospital.' There was no particular reason why Megan should have heard from Sonia, they hadn't been close. But what had happened two weeks after Sonia had left her job, the cancelled wedding and the missing groom, had been a talking point for months.

The smile slid from Jaye's face for a moment. 'I haven't been in contact with Sonia since then, either.'

Which meant he hadn't been in contact with his child, either. Megan knew exactly what it was like to be the unwanted child of a rich and influential man, who had no scruples about rewriting history whenever it suited him. Maybe that was why she wanted to slap Jaye now. Not for Sonia, but for the child.

'I heard she had a baby.'

A pulse beat at the side of his temple. 'That's what I heard, too.'

A baby who had no place here. If Jay hadn't turned suddenly, in response to his name being called, Megan thought she might have slapped him. There was no excuse now. He knew he was a father, and clearly he'd decided that was a technicality that he could afford to overlook.

'I'm sorry…' When he turned back his face was impassive. 'I have to go, it seems that lunch is ready. I hope we'll be able to speak more later.'

Then he was gone, helping John Ferris to chivvy everyone through to the next room for lunch. Megan waited for the press of people to thin a little and slipped out of the room, turning left instead of right, and making her way back to the great entrance hall and up the stairs.

Jaye had remembered Megan as soon as he'd seen her application form. The nurse who could always coax a smile from her patients. Her enthusiasm for the work of his charity had shone through her answers to the carefully worded questions on the application form, and after he'd interviewed her, John Ferris had agreed that Megan was the one candidate who stood out from all the rest.

He'd wondered whether Megan would remember him,

and, despite the awkwardness of the situation, rather hoped she would. When Megan had replied within the hour to the email inviting her here, he'd supposed that either she was inclined to overlook the most damning and humiliating episode in his life, or that he'd made much less of an impression on her than she'd had on him.

Wrong. On both counts. When he'd scanned the room for her, his heart beating a little faster at the remembered warmth of her blue eyes, he'd found only ice. And her pointed remark about Sonia told him that she remembered him all too well, and that she was inclined to overlook nothing.

There was time. Four days was more than enough time to gauge her feelings, and talk about it. Jaye's gaze rested on the empty seat at the dining table. It was possible that Megan had taken some time out from the group to decide what to throw at him next, but he doubted it. When he'd seen her working on the wards, he'd been impressed with the way that she sized up a situation, took decisions and then acted on them.

'Have you seen Megan Wheeler?' He buttonholed one of the teenagers from the village, who'd been co-opted to help show everyone to their rooms. 'Blue jacket. White top with a...' He waved his hand to indicate the soft folds of Megan's blouse.

Emma smirked. 'That's called a cowl neckline.'

'I thought you'd be the one to ask about that. Have you seen her?'

'No.'

Jaye turned, hurrying from the room, a sudden anger biting at his heart. If Megan wanted to walk out, that was her decision. But he was damned if she was going to make it on the basis of what she'd heard about him and Sonia, because that was almost certainly a lie.

* * *

The retractable handle of her case wasn't pushed down far enough, and Megan was struggling to get it into the boot of her car. She turned as she heard the scrunch of gravel under Jaye's feet.

'Leaving so soon?' He decided to confine his opening salvo to the obvious facts.

'Yes.'

'This course isn't an optional extra. We're expecting all of our new employees to complete it.'

'I understand that. I've made my decision.' He thought he saw scorn in Megan's eyes. Such beautiful eyes, blue and clear, and apparently unable to hide her feelings. He liked that.

'And…clearly I'm a factor in that decision.'

'Yes.' Her lip curled, and Jaye suppressed the impulse to smile. In a world where people tended to tell him what they thought he wanted to hear, this was almost refreshing.

'I don't suppose you'd care to elaborate on that?'

She pulled the case out of the open boot and pushed the handle down. Jaye resisted the impulse to help her as she heaved the case back into the boot and slammed it shut. Then she turned to face him.

'I'm looking for an employer who I can trust. That's non-negotiable.'

'It's non-negotiable for us, too. I think we should talk about this, Megan.'

'There's nothing *to* talk about. Actions speak louder than words.'

Jaye was blocking her path to the driver's door and she walked round him, getting into the car. He jumped as she wrenched the door shut, slamming it hard, as if to demonstrate her point.

A frisson of *How dare she?* melted into the irrational impulse to beg, if that was what it would take to make Megan stop. Jaye walked around to the front of the car, planting his hands on the bonnet. Megan glared at him, and he wondered for a moment whether he'd made a mistake and she was capable of driving straight over him.

'Is it going to hurt you so much to listen? Because if it does, you've made a good decision.'

Here, outside the public part of the house, it was impossible that someone wasn't watching, and now that he had to raise his voice to make himself heard, they were probably listening, too. But however much it dug at his pride to be seen blocking her path to prevent her from leaving, he couldn't give up now.

'We want medical professionals who can listen to other people—' Megan cut him short by suddenly winding down the window and leaning out.

'I think you should know that appealing to my professional pride isn't going to work.'

It seemed to be working. Megan was no longer scrunching her face up in a scowl, which was a distinct improvement. The feeble winter sunshine tangled in the gold of her hair, making him feel as if he were looking at an angry angel.

'Noted. Let's make it personal, then. I'll get on my knees if that's what you want…' *That* would provide a talking point for whoever was watching.

The ghost of a smile flitted across her face. 'That would be embarrassing for both of us.'

If Megan was the woman he thought she was, there was no risk in what he was about to do. All the same, Jaye felt a slight tremor in his chest. He'd been wrong before, and he didn't relish the idea of explaining how he'd let one of the best candidates the charity had seen in years slip through their fingers, without putting up more of a fight.

'All right, then. If you can face the idea that you might be wrong, we'll go inside and talk. If not, have a nice life.'

He turned, making for the path that led around the side of the house. Jaye felt his heart clench with inappropriate joy as he heard the car door open and then close again, and Megan's footsteps behind him.

Walking down the stone steps that led to the semi-basement kitchen, Jaye opened the door for Megan and she walked inside. Now that lunch had been served the place was deserted, but there were still enough cups left in the dresser to throw a few if Megan got the urge. He motioned her towards the large kitchen table and she sat down.

'Coffee?' Something hot, to break the ice.

'Yes. Thank you.'

He made the coffee, aware of her gaze on his back. The silence was killing him. It gave Jaye time to want things, to consider telling Megan everything. How he'd loved Sonia, but it had turned out that the thing she'd really loved had been the idea of being a duchess, and all that brought. How diminished he felt, every time someone looked straight through him and found only his title.

He put the mugs on the table and sat down opposite her. Despite the warmth in there, Megan was still wrapped in her coat, as if she was leaving herself prepared for a quick exit. But her gaze never moved from his face. Frank, blue eyes which would have made confiding in her easy, if only he had the nerve to do it.

She took a sip of her coffee. 'I'm listening.'

CHAPTER TWO

WOULD SHE EVEN be here if she hadn't seen the burst of passion in his dark eyes? If thought and action hadn't blended deliciously into one as he'd marched around to the front of her car, blocking her way. Megan didn't want to think about it.

But he was right. It was a surprise to find that Jaye even cared what she thought, but since he'd made it plain that he did, the least she could do was to listen. If it turned out that his reasons for treating his child like an optional extra were anything like her own father's, then she'd leave.

'I'm not going to pretend that I don't know what this is about. I'm well aware that what happened between Sonia and me was a talking point at the hospital where you both worked.'

'That you left three days before the wedding. And that she was pregnant.' Megan tried to keep the accusatory tone from her voice. The facts spoke for themselves.

'Yes. That story is…basically true.'

Then what were they doing, sitting here talking about it? Megan swallowed down her exasperation.

'What you do is entirely your business. But it's my business who I choose to work for, and I want that to be someone who I feel I can trust.'

'I admire that sentiment. Not everyone would stick to

their principles and give up something they want in favour of something they think is right.'

'I'm just being practical. If I'm going to be working abroad, I need to know that there's a support network here that I can rely on. That's non-negotiable for me.'

It should be non-negotiable for anyone, but Megan felt it more keenly. When she'd been little, 'Uncle' Harry had visited once every two weeks, bearing expensive toys and presents. It hadn't been until she'd been a teenager that she'd found out that he was really her father, and she'd spent the intervening years trying to distance herself from his brash attempts to have a say in her future. She wasn't going to allow all that to count for nothing by putting herself in a position where a man just like Harry could tell her what to do.

Jaye's gaze caught hers. Dark, and almost tender. 'The story was true, but it left out some important details. I wasn't the father of Sonia's child.'

'But…' Megan took a swig of her coffee and almost choked on it. 'So you just walked away…?'

'I'm sure you're not naïve enough to imagine that there wasn't any *just* about it. We had a few full and frank discussions.' He hesitated, as if he might be about to elaborate, and then shook his head. 'The only other thing you need to know is that I left because Sonia called off the wedding.'

'I don't…' Megan covered her mouth with her hand. Actually, she *did* believe him.

'You don't think I'm telling you the truth?' He shrugged. 'I'm afraid I can't help you with that. You'll have to make up your own mind.'

If he'd been lying he probably would have elaborated, or used his charm to convince her. But his face was impassive, making the sadness in his beautiful eyes even more compelling.

'But you must have known what everyone at the hospital

was saying. Didn't you want to correct it?' It would have been easy enough. A ten-minute call to one of the hospital bosses, who would have passed the information on to his secretary, with the hint that it could be tactfully fed to one or two other people. That was how rumours worked.

'Yes, I knew exactly what Sonia's friends were saying. And, no, I made no effort to correct it, even though I knew it was untrue.'

Discretion maybe. Or maybe he just didn't care what anyone else thought. Jaye had always seemed quite capable of that kind of arrogance. Or maybe humbled pride, that any woman could cheat on him.

It didn't matter. She wasn't thinking of making Jaye her best friend, she was looking for a boss who she could trust.

'I believed what I heard and…' Megan felt herself redden at the thought. 'I'm sorry. I should have known better than to trust second-hand gossip.'

He shrugged her apology away. 'What you heard was as much my responsibility as Sonia's. What matters now is that you make your decision based on the facts.' He smiled and Megan felt herself flush, heat zinging up her spine.

He hadn't given her a shred of proof, and precious little explanation, but she believed him. If those eyes were lying then she could kiss goodbye to everything she thought she knew about human nature.

'I still have a decision to make?' Megan heard herself whisper the words. If Jaye couldn't forgive her behaviour, she wouldn't blame him.

He planted his forearms on the table, hands clasped together, and leaned towards her. Challenging, and yet intimate too. 'Absolutely. I believe you'll justify my confidence in you.'

'Then…' Megan's head was spinning, and her heart was pumping fast. Both organs seemed to be vying for their say in the matter. 'I like working for people who expect success. They generally put fewer limitations on their goals.'

Jaye laughed suddenly. 'I'm glad to hear that.'

He clinked his mug against hers, and drank. A toast to an unexpected success, dragged from the jaws of failure. If nothing else, working for Jaye's charity was going to be interesting, and even more of a challenge than Megan had thought.

If Jaye did nothing else in the next four days, at least he might manage to repair some of the damage. His and Sonia's engagement might have been a disaster in the making, averted only at the very last minute, but there was no reason why Megan's career should be damaged by the fallout.

He hadn't examined the potential consequences of letting the rumours persist, wanting only to disappear. Hurt and feeling that if he shrunk any more, he'd lose himself completely, he'd retreated to Sri Lanka. The clinic that his father had founded after the 2005 tsunami, and which Jaye had helped build, was a place of tranquillity and calm. A place to heal and find his balance.

But it was a different balance. He'd tried dating again, but had found himself caught up in a fury of mistrust, unable to accept that his new partner's motives for being with him could be any different from Sonia's. In the end, he'd given up the struggle and had let her go, burying himself once more in the work that brought him peace and fulfilment.

Jaye stared at the crackling logs in the fireplace. When Megan had believed him, it had felt as if a little piece of his heart had been repaired. Here, sitting in his apartment, with only the sound of the fire to keep him company, he knew that one piece would never be enough.

He should get some sleep. Tomorrow was going to be a

full day, and he needed to focus. Preferably on something other than Megan's smile.

The conference was under way, and already it felt to Megan that she'd entered a self-sufficient bubble. One that brought people who'd worked in many different parts of the world together with those who were just starting out on their careers. It was almost impossible to find the time to meet and talk to everyone.

But the one person she never seemed to talk to was Jaye. Although he was always there, he was always at the opposite end of the room from her. The coincidences were beginning to form a pattern.

At least she could watch him, and that had its very definite pleasures. Tall, graceful and always impeccably dressed, he was the stuff that daydreams were made of. And if he caught her watching him, then that could surely only be because he was watching her.

Jaye had retreated to his apartment in the west wing of the building, and sat in his study with John Ferris. It had been an exhausting two days.

'You're pleased with how things are going?'

'On the whole.' John sank into the leather chair on the other side of the fireplace. 'I was a bit disappointed about Steven.'

Jaye and John had spent over two hours last night with the young doctor, talking through all of his reasons for leaving. 'But you did say that was the point of this. That we shouldn't assume any particular outcome for any particular candidate but find out what the best way forward was.'

John nodded. 'Yeah. Steven's not in the right place to take up a job with us at the moment. He's got a lot of potential, though, and I want to keep in touch with him.'

'You think that in twenty years' time he'll be Head of Surgery somewhere. Consulting for us, and mentoring our young surgeons?'

'Who knows? We have to look towards the long term, and funnier things have happened.'

This was exactly why Jaye had recruited John. Four years ago, Jaye had returned from Sri Lanka with a new commitment for a future that had seemed empty without a wife and the prospect of children. It was time to take a step back from his private practice in London and concentrate on the charity that he and his father had built together. And he had needed an organiser, someone who could work side by side with him and run the charity, while Jaye concentrated on its medical activities. John had been that person.

'What about Megan?' John's question interrupted his reverie.

'What…about her?' Megan had occupied his thoughts for much of the last two days, and that was a very good reason to take a step back. John's decisions would be far less clouded by the urgent need to look into her eyes and see her smile.

'It looked as if *she* was intent on leaving the other day, before you threw yourself in front of her car in the driveway. I asked her if everything was all right.'

'What did she say?'

John laughed. 'She played her cards as close to her chest as you are now. Told me that it was a misunderstanding, and that you'd come to her rescue. She made it very clear that it was all her fault and that you'd addressed her concerns very fully.'

Jaye resisted the impulse to smile. Since he hadn't spoken with Megan himself in the course of the last two days, he'd relied on her demeanour and the few shy smiles that she'd given, when his gaze had met hers. It felt good to hear that Megan was moving forward on the basis that she really did believe him.

'It wasn't all her fault. Mostly it was mine.'

'Yeah. Takes two to tango.' John was looking at him steadily. 'Is there anything else I should know? You and her?'

The question knocked Jaye off balance for a moment. Maybe because he'd wondered more than once how it might have been had he met Megan before Sonia. But the truth of it was that the only moments of intimacy between them had been in his head.

'No. Megan and I met before, years ago and in the course of our jobs. But that's all, there's never been anything between us.'

'In that case… I wonder how you feel about offering her a posting in Sri Lanka. They're short-staffed there and, with the new doctor in residence still settling in, they could do with the help.' John flashed Jaye a questioning look.

'Staffing's your province, John. I trust your judgement.'

'And I appreciate that. But considering your close ties with the clinic in Sri Lanka, I thought I'd get your opinion before I mentioned the idea to Megan.'

'I think it's a great idea. I'd like to see what Megan makes of Sri Lanka.'

Megan trudged across the well-manicured lawn, sliding down the steep slope to the edge of the woodlands beyond, where Jaye's father was shovelling clumps of sticky earth into a wheelbarrow.

'Megan…' Raj Perera straightened up, leaning on his spade as she approached. 'You've decided on a walk?'

'No.' Megan pulled the piece of paper from her coat pocket. 'I was wondering if you could help me with something.'

'Of course. That's my role as your group leader this weekend. And I could do with a break.'

Megan handed over the paper, and Raj looked at it. 'John's set us all a challenge. We all have to give a five-minute talk about one of our charity's programmes. I've been given the Western Province Free Clinic in Sri Lanka.'

'That's a place very close to my heart.' Raj's way of making an observation, then watching and waiting to see what you'd do with it, was a lot like Jaye's. A little less disturbing maybe, because Megan didn't have to contend with her own quickening heartbeat, which happened whenever Jaye was around.

'I heard that you and your wife were the ones who started it.'

'Yes, we did.'

'Well... I asked John if there were any restrictions on how we could get the information we needed and he said there weren't. And since you were there, right at the start...'

Raj thought for a moment, and then nodded. 'What do you have in mind?'

'I thought maybe a short interview, if you could spare the time.' Megan gestured towards the spade. 'I can do some digging in return...'

Raj's smile reminded her of Jaye's too, but it was a lot more freely given. 'Very well. What would you like to know?'

'Why you founded the clinic.' Megan took the spade and started to dig.

'Caroline and I were in Sri Lanka, visiting relatives, when the tsunami hit in 2005. Many people needed medical aid, and we immediately gave what help we could. I set up a clinic in a tent, under a tree.'

'And people came...?' The earth was sticky and unyielding and Megan heaved her weight onto the spade to sink it into the ground.

'Yes, they came. There were so many, and sometimes they only had the clothes they stood up in. Caroline helped organise the effort to feed and clothe them and give them some kind of roof over their heads.'

'It must have been…heartbreaking.' Megan had worked in areas of great need, but never in a disaster zone.

'It was. And yet it warmed my heart too. Jaye is my oldest son, I have three more. All four of them came, for six weeks, to give what help they could.'

'That must have made you very proud.'

'It did. Each of them has followed their own path, but Jaye… In that six weeks he found his calling.'

Until recently, Megan would have thought that Jaye Perera's only calling in life was to make money, and exercise the power that he had inherited. Raj was clearly not referring to either of those things.

'His calling? To be a doctor, you mean?'

Raj smiled. 'He'd already walked that path—Jaye had just qualified as a doctor. He was evaluating his next step, and had a number of very good options available to him here in the UK. But he gave them up and stayed in Sri Lanka for a year, working with me to build the clinic.'

'He raised funds?' This was a new side of Jaye, which Megan hadn't seen before.

'No, he *built* the clinic. He helped dig the foundations, and then poured concrete and laid bricks. And every afternoon he cleaned up and worked at our ramshackle surgery. Accuse me of bias if you wish, but I've never seen a man work so hard.'

This definitely wasn't the Jaye that Megan knew. She'd come to terms with the idea of him as someone who made things happen, and that many of those things were for the benefit of others. But getting his hands dirty? Megan had never, even in her wildest dreams, pictured that.

'I didn't realise. He seems…so different.'

'Maybe you just don't know him very well.'

Maybe, maybe not. But the tantalising glimpses of what Jaye had been put a new and puzzling perspective on the man that he seemed to be now.

'Tell me about the challenges.' Megan straightened, surveying her handiwork. The small dent in the ground put the task of digging foundations sharply into perspective. 'Um… Medical first. Then social…'

CHAPTER THREE

JAYE SAT AT the back of the group of chairs in the room that had been set aside for the conference activities. Everyone had done well, and each of the five-minute talks was obviously carefully crafted.

Megan stood up, clutching her laptop, and walked to the front of the group, plugging in the cable that led to the screen behind her. A number of people had already displayed photographs to accompany their talks, and Jaye wondered which ones she'd chosen.

'I've decided to make my presentation in the form of an interview. I'd like to thank Dr and Mrs Perera for all the help they've given me, and for agreeing to talk about the early days of the Western Province Free Clinic…'

Jaye could hardly suppress a grin. There was no better way to tell the story of the clinic than to use his father and mother's own words.

'I'm not sure that's quite what was intended.' A voice sounded from the centre of the group.

Jaye was pretty sure that was exactly what was intended. The tasks that John had set here weren't quite as straightforward as they looked, and this one was clearly about methods, just as much as results.

Megan looked around the audience, reddening a little, and Jaye suppressed the urge to come to her defence.

'Our remit was to find out as much as we could. Which I've done.'

'You're missing the point…' Rob was the young doctor whose voice was always loudest in the group discussions, which was a shame, because his vision seemed always the most limited.

'Which point?' Megan softened her question with a smile, and Jaye wondered privately what Rob had done to deserve that particular burst of sunshine.

'You have to do the research and come up with your own answers. You can't just ask someone else, that's not in the rules…' Rob gave a sigh of exasperation, as if he were talking to a recalcitrant child.

Enough. If Rob wanted to throw his weight around, he could do it with *him*, not Megan. Jaye moved to intervene but Megan was already replying.

'Isn't asking someone who was there the best kind of research there is? I'm not aware of any rule against it.'

'The only rules were the ones that everyone chose to superimpose on themselves.' John was grinning broadly as he cut in. 'Let's see your presentation, Megan.'

Jaye breathed a silent *thank you* and settled back in his chair. It had been entirely inappropriate to want to defend Megan, but the impulse still lingered, like an uninvited guest at a party.

Megan was speaking again, and then she tapped a key on her laptop and sat down. His mother and father appeared on the screen, seated together at the kitchen table in their apartment.

'Dr and Mrs Perera, you were in Sri Lanka when the tsunami of 2005 hit.' Megan's voice came from somewhere behind the camera. 'The medical station that you set up to help the sick and the injured was the foundation of the present-day clinic. What were the biggest problems you faced…?'

The video lasted exactly five minutes. By the time it had finished, Jaye felt tears pricking at the sides of his eyes.

This wasn't appropriate either. He knew the story well enough, he'd been there for much of it. The interview had clearly been carefully edited, and somehow Megan had managed to catch all the passion, the battle against seemingly overwhelming odds, and the achievements that had kept everyone going. At the end of the interview there were photographs, some of which had been taken from his parents' personal albums.

There was silence in the room and then someone started to clap. Megan grabbed her laptop and hurried back to her seat, red-faced, as everyone applauded.

Everyone had crowded around Megan when the session ended, wanting to know more about the Sri Lankan clinic. Jaye had hurried from the room, trying not to notice that Megan's head had turned to watch him go.

He'd taken refuge in an armchair, tucked into the corner of the large landing where the main staircase split in two. It was one of his favourite places in the house where he could sit and watch the world go by, without being a part of it. But as Megan walked through the hallway, she looked up and saw him there.

'May I join you?' She walked half way up towards him and then stopped.

'Yes, of course.' Jaye rose from the chair and sat down on the stairs next to it.

'Is this *your* stair?' She had a mischievous look in her eyes as she approached him.

Actually, it was. The one where he'd sat as a child, hidden from the hallway by the turn in the stairs but able to peep out and see what was going on.

'Why don't you try it for size?' There was plenty of room there for two.

Megan nodded, sitting down next to him. Looking around, she peered through the heavy banister rails to see down into the main hall.

'It's a good stair. Just right.' She smiled at him, and Jaye felt a warm tingle shoot down his spine.

'I think so.' His legs were a little longer now, so it wasn't such a good hiding place as it had once been. But his initials were still there, carved into the stair tread and hidden by the carpet.

She was hugging her laptop, obviously there on a mission. Jaye waited. No doubt Megan would come out with it, sooner rather than later.

'I hope you didn't mind… Your mother and father were really happy to do the interview and they offered to let me scan some of their photographs… They were very kind, and I didn't mean to impose on them by asking so much. I hope you don't feel it was too personal.'

'Not a bit. And my parents looked as if they were really enjoying it. My father never passes up a chance to reminisce.' It occurred to Jaye that including his parents' words and photographs hadn't been an exercise in currying favour. Megan had simply gone down the route that she felt told the story best, despite not being sure whether he'd approve. The thought made him smile.

'I had to cut some bits out.' She looked up at him, her eyes bright. 'Did you really help dig the foundations of the clinic?'

'I was a lot younger then.' It seemed like a hundred years ago. And yet somehow he could still touch the feeling of something fresh and new.

'John spoke to me about sending me there for my first assignment. I'll have to check out your bricklaying skills.'

She was clearly testing the water, waiting for Jaye's opinion on the matter.

'Well, when you get there, take the path that runs around the back of the building. We all put our initials in the cement, under the window of the main ward.'

Megan gave a broad smile. 'I will. I can't wait…'

She seemed to have said all she'd come to say and had begun to fidget nervously. Jaye stretched his legs out in front of him, wondering if he might persuade her to stay. Just so he could breathe her scent a little longer.

'What do you think of the course so far?'

'It's been great, really helpful. It's been good to talk to people from other charities and compare the different approaches. And being in this house has made all the difference.'

Jaye had always felt he paled into insignificance next to the great house, set in its spectacular landscape, but it was disappointing to hear the words on Megan's lips. He wouldn't have minded so much if Sonia hadn't fallen so irrevocably in love with the place. When he'd first brought her here, she'd hardly looked at him all day, as if he'd suddenly melted into a poor second place in her heart. Jaye had tried to dismiss the feeling, but it had turned out to be a warning of things to come.

'You think the *house* is what makes the difference. Not the people in it?'

She flashed him a withering look, as if he'd misunderstood on purpose. 'What I meant was that we don't leave every evening, so we sit and talk a lot more. Don't you think that surroundings have an impact on how people operate?'

Jaye chuckled. 'Yes, I do. It's one of the founding principles of the clinic in Sri Lanka. We tried to make it a quiet place, where people could find healing and balance.'

'The principles of Ayurvedic medicine? You practise that?'

'No. But we understand that tradition sometimes has a lot to offer. We respect it.'

Megan nodded. 'Everything I hear about the clinic in Sri Lanka just makes me want to go even more…'

She'd relaxed now, her shoulder brushing his arm as she turned to put her laptop on the stair next to her. That one touch seemed to linger.

'So what impact do you think this house has had on the way the group has operated?'

'Apart from the fact that I'm tempted to take a sandwich with me when I trek from my bed over to the shower in the mornings…? Not that my room isn't lovely, of course, and very comfortable.'

'Of course. And leaving your early morning hunger pangs out of it?' Jaye filed the information under the category of irrelevant but nice to know.

'It's like a bubble. It seems as if it's been here for ever, and it must have seen so much over the years. That makes almost anything possible.'

Jaye swallowed hard. She seemed to have reached into him and found his own response to the house he'd been brought up in. Megan had seen past the glitz and the glamour that seemed to preoccupy so many others.

'These are all the past Dukes?' She was pointing up at the portraits, which stretched along the landing and up the stairs.

'Yes, that's right.'

'And you're carrying on their tradition.'

'Not necessarily.' Jaye heard his own laugh, almost breathless in the bubble that Megan had created around the two of them. 'Some of them were rogues. The one just there almost gambled the estate away. Luckily for us, his son was a little more prudent. He's the next one along.'

Megan craned her neck, staring at the painting and then

glanced back at Jaye. 'I can see a likeness, I think… Between you and the son.'

'I'd be proud if there was one. He was one of the more enlightened Dukes of Marlowe.'

'Why?' She turned and Jaye shivered in her steady gaze. 'What did he do?'

'He was a campaigner against social injustice, at a time when no one thought about the sufferings of working people. He put his principles into practice, here on the estate.'

'You're very lucky, to have someone like that in your family.'

That was what his father had taught Jaye. When he'd been barely old enough to understand, his father had told him that this collection of paintings was a reminder of the choices that he could make in his own life.

'We all have someone in our family we can look up to, don't we?'

'No. We don't.' Megan was shaking her head, quirking her mouth down.

If anything was possible, surely Jaye could ask her what made her so sure of that. But he didn't dare.

'I'm very lucky, then. My father's always been someone I could look up to.'

'Yes, you are.' She puffed out a breath, as if whatever was on her mind didn't matter so much after all, and she may as well say it. 'Me and my father aren't close, and that suits me fine. He had an affair with my mother—he was married and she was his secretary. I'm his awkward little secret.'

There was a weary defiance in her tone, as if she were challenging him to think whatever he liked. It occurred to Jaye that saying he was sorry to hear it would be quite the wrong thing to do.

'Not so much of the *little*, I think…'

She stared at him for a moment, and then suddenly laughed. 'Thank you. I don't consider myself as *little* either, although I wouldn't be surprised if my father did. He has a multi-million-pound business to run and much bigger fish to fry.'

It was one more piece in a puzzle that he was becoming compelled to complete. It really had been personal when Megan had walked out on him that first day. She'd thought he was like her own father, and that tough, personal experience had lent an edge to her anger.

'And you don't want any part of that?'

'No, I don't. I don't like secrets, and this is his secret, not mine.'

Jaye called her bluff. 'What's his name? Maybe I've heard of him…'

Megan laughed, shaking her head. 'Maybe you have, if you read the financial pages in the paper. And I'm not telling you, he has a wife and two sons. It wouldn't be fair to them.'

He could respect that. All the same, it seemed that Megan was more burdened by the secret than she let on. But there was no chance to ask any more.

Voices sounded, growing louder as the group started to straggle back into the conference room, some still carrying their coffee with them. Megan sprang to her feet, looking around as if someone was going to appear out of nowhere and admonish her for sitting here, talking.

'I've got to go…'

'I'll be along in a minute.' Jaye suppressed the urge to tell her that this was his home, and she could sit here and talk with him for as long as she liked. She was already half-way down the stairs, clutching her laptop across her chest.

He watched through the bannisters as she joined the first of the group to appear in the hallway. Much as he had when he'd been a child, watching the guests arrive at one of his parents' parties.

Jaye craned his neck, watching the top of Megan's head disappear. He was no child now, and some possibilities were no longer a part of his future. He'd been scarred by love, and Megan was just making those scars ache a little.

Every time Megan caught a glimpse of the man behind Jaye's façade it felt as if she were being swallowed up in the softness of his eyes. As if just talking to him was dangerous and exciting—something secret and delicious. And hadn't she just been telling him how she abhorred secrets?

She had to get a grip. Talking was exactly what they were supposed to be doing. People were meant to swap experiences and ideas at this conference, that was the whole point of it.

But she still couldn't resist looking for him, knowing where he was in the room and what he was doing. Even if she caught just a glimpse of him, it made the floor lurch under her feet, and gave her that sickening feeling that everything was spinning out of control.

It was almost a relief to find that he wasn't joining in with the group discussions the following morning, as he was helping with the arrangements for the party that evening. But it was only a brief respite.

There was music swelling from one corner of the ballroom, where a string quartet was playing. Four young women in black dresses were clearly having some fun, inserting their own improvisations into some well-known classical pieces. Flickering candles highlighted the sheen of sumptuous fabric that hung at the high glazed doors leading out onto the terrace. Suddenly it all paled into insignificance.

Jaye.

In a dark suit and a crisp white shirt, which was currently goading Megan's imagination into some very bad thoughts indeed. It was a twist on the ultimate embarrassment, those dreams where she walked into a crowded place and found herself naked. Imagining the smooth ripple of Jaye's skin made her feel even more exposed.

The room was beginning to fill up, people she knew from the course, along with a legion of other guests, who all seemed to know each other. Megan swallowed hard and marched over to the drinks table. Caroline Perera turned and gave a smiling compliment about her hair and dress, including Megan in the group that she was talking to.

After making sure that everyone had a drink, and that they had all been introduced to each other, Caroline slipped away, greeting more people and introducing them. Megan smiled at the slim, shy-looking man standing next to her, who looked as if he'd just wandered in off the street and stayed for drinks.

'Is this your first time? Working abroad?' The man smiled back.

'No, I was in Africa for a year. I came back four months ago, and I've been working as a supply nurse since then.'

'Africa?' The man's eyes lit up. 'Which part? I'm just back from Rwanda...'

Tim Gregson was fascinating. He must have been involved in aid work at a high level because his comments were insightful and informed, but he seemed intent on grilling Megan on her experiences and finding out what she thought.

'You've been to so many places. What exactly do you do?' Megan tried again to turn the conversation back to Tim's experiences.

'Oh... I advise. People listen sometimes.' Tim shrugged

vaguely and Megan stiffened suddenly as a quiet laugh came from behind her.

'Tim's a parliamentary special advisor. He has his finger on the pulse at Westminster.' Jaye stepped into Megan's line of view, reaching forward to shake Tim's hand warmly.

'If only. I'm not sure that anyone has enough fingers for that…' Tim chuckled, clearly pleased with Jaye's assertion.

'A voice of sanity, then?' Jaye shot a sidelong grin at Megan, and she felt a rush of embarrassment. It happened every time. That delicious and yet horribly out-of-control feeling as she stumbled and fell into the warmth of his gaze.

'That would be nice. Sometimes I wonder,' Tim responded dryly, and Jaye laughed. Clearly the two men knew each other well. Maybe they wouldn't notice if she slipped away.

She took a tentative step backwards and Jaye rounded on her. 'Tim's far too self-effacing. He's helped us out with the planning on a lot of our projects.'

'Caroline doesn't see things that way,' Tim joked. 'She frisked me on the way in to make sure I wasn't carrying any sharp objects.'

Jaye chuckled. 'My mother has a much longer memory than I have.'

'Ask him about the sticking plaster.' Tim leaned confidingly towards Megan. 'I'll lay odds he hasn't forgotten about that one.'

'Sticking plaster?' Megan forgot all about escape and turned to Jaye.

'That was a very long time ago. When we were kids we decided to try our hands at covert surveillance, like we'd seen on TV. We rigged up a couple of voice recorders and taped them under our shirts…'

'With the biggest roll of sticking plaster I'd ever seen.

Jaye had obviously been taking lessons from his father about how to tape broken ribs, and was extremely thorough…'

'I think I still have the scars from where my mother ripped it all off to see what was underneath.' Jaye's hand wandered to his chest, and Megan swallowed down the impulse to remind him that she was a nurse and could take a look at them if he wanted.

'The worst thing was that we never actually managed to record anything. We'd put our jumpers and coats on, to hide all the lumps and bumps, and all you could hear was a bit of rustling, and then Caroline, asking us what on earth we were up to.'

Jaye quirked the sides of his mouth down. 'Yes. That was a big disappointment.'

The image of two boys, play-acting and exploring in the winding corridors and vast rooms, floated into Megan's mind. The Jaye who made use of the formal entrance and main staircase seemed to have lost something along the way. Or maybe it had been stolen from him. It seemed that Sonia had a lot to answer for.

'More wine?' Tim turned and picked up a bottle from the table.

'No…thanks.' Megan shielded the top of her glass with her hand. 'I should go and see where Alice has got to…' She looked around desperately, hoping that the friend she'd made during the conference wasn't anywhere in sight.

Jaye was suddenly still and silent, as if this sudden glimpse at something like intimacy was too much for him too. Megan smiled at Tim and made her escape.

CHAPTER FOUR

MEGAN LOOKED STUNNING. So much so that Jaye had forgotten to issue the expected compliment about her appearance. She wore a plain dark blue dress, the sheen of which didn't come close to matching the sheen of her hair, which was caught up loosely at the back of her head. High heels made her legs look even longer than they actually were. The only jewellery she wore, a heavy twisted silver bangle, was obviously one of a kind. She made everyone else here look as if they'd tried far too hard, and in doing so had lost the sartorial plot.

The string quartet had thrown off the precision of Bach and begun to play a selection of popular songs, all with their very own distinctive flavour. In response, Jaye's father had spun his mother into an empty space at one end of the ballroom, creating an impromptu dancing area.

The idea that Jaye might do the same with Megan was… impossible. He wanted too much from her. Her scent. The feel of her hand on his shoulder. That slightly dizzy feeling that her smile engendered.

'Very nice party.' Tim broke his reverie.

'Thanks. There are a few people I'd like you to meet…' Jaye resolved the need to mingle with his suspicion that Tim would be standing alone in a corner of the room if he left him here. Tim didn't do small talk, and if he'd found him with anyone other than Megan, it would have been a surprise to find his friend so relaxed and at ease.

'Uh… Later? I'm getting a headache, I don't suppose you have any paracetamol, do you?'

'In the box in the kitchen. You know where the key is. Are you all right?'

Tim shot him a pained look. 'Yes, I'm fine. Stop being such a doctor and go and do your duty as a host…'

Out of the range of Jaye's smile Megan had begun to relax again. She'd found Alice and they'd joined the group of new friends, laughing and talking by the fireplace. It was almost an hour before Megan saw Jaye heading towards them, a bottle of red in one hand and a bottle of white in the other, obviously intent on refilling their glasses.

She slipped away. A little cool air on her face, maybe some water, would dispel the heat that she felt rising to her cheeks.

A few wrong turns and she found her way downstairs to the kitchen. The light was on, and Megan looked around, wondering if she'd disturbed someone else who was intent on escape.

No one. Megan fetched a glass from the cupboard and held it under the tap. Then the sound of a rasped breath reached her ears.

She jumped, looking around. Still no one. Maybe this place was haunted, only that wouldn't account for anything because she didn't believe in ghosts. She walked to the far end of the room, to a brick archway, finding that it led into a small alcove with a couple of easy chairs and a table.

Tim was sitting in one of the chairs, a half-empty glass of water and an open packet of paracetamol on the table in front of him. His eyes were closed and his breathing seemed laboured.

It occurred to Megan that maybe this was one last challenge, designed to test the group of doctors and nurses. But Jaye and Tim would hardly stage such a thing here, and anyway the conference was over now. When she walked over to Tim, touching the back of his hand, his eyes flickered open.

'Megan…? What's the matter?'

'Are you all right?' She didn't wait for an answer, leaning forward to lay her hand on Tim's forehead. He was burning up.

'Just a twenty-four-hour flu bug. I thought I'd got the better of it, but it seems to have come on again. I'll be okay in a minute—go back to the party.' Tim reached groggily for the packet of paracetamol and Megan snatched it up from the table. Two tablets had already been broken from the blister pack, and if Tim had taken them she didn't want him taking any more.

'Will you stay here? Just for one moment?'

'Yeah. Yeah, no problem.' Tim's eyes fluttered closed again. Megan turned, hurrying through the kitchen and upstairs to the ballroom. In a room which held more than its share of doctors, there was only one she wanted to find.

Jaye felt Megan's touch on his arm, and the warm shiver that ran down his spine suddenly froze when he saw the look on her face. 'Please come. It's Tim, he's ill.'

'What's the matter? He was complaining of a headache earlier…' Jaye dumped the bottle he was holding on the mantelpiece and followed Megan, who was already making her way back out of the room.

'He says it's a twenty-four-hour flu. I'm not so sure about that.'

Jaye was much more disposed to trust Megan's assessment of the situation than Tim's. She stopped as she reached the main hallway, looking right and then left.

'Where is he?'

'In the main kitchen, downstairs.'

'This way…' Jaye laid his hand lightly on her back to guide her in the right direction, without thinking, feeling her jump as he touched her. Even now, as they hurried down to the kitchen, electricity was zinging in the air.

She led him to the snug room next to the kitchen. Tim was slumped in one of the chairs, and focussed his eyes on them with difficulty.

'Oh, no… You didn't bring the cavalry, did you?'

'I'm afraid I did.' Megan smiled at Tim and then turned to Jaye. 'He had this open packet of paracetamol, and he's obviously had some water. I don't know what he's already taken, so I stopped him from taking any more.'

'Okay. There's a log in the medicine cabinet. Sit with him while I check.' Jaye took the blister pack from her hand, walking back into the kitchen.

When he returned, Megan was sitting on the low table in front of Tim. She'd pushed his cuff back and curled her fingers around his wrist. The clock on the mantelpiece ticked loudly in the silence.

'Your pulse is steady. Maybe a little fast.' Megan's warmth was like a tangible presence in the room, and Jaye almost envied his friend.

She was making no fuss, using her own observations to guide her. Jaye knew it was exactly the right approach to take with Tim, but Megan seemed to have come to that conclusion after only a brief conversation with him.

'You don't want to catch this… I thought I had it licked, but it's got a sting in its tail.' Tim managed to summon up some of his former determination to be left alone, and Megan thwarted it with a look of mild rebuke.

'You said earlier you were just back from Africa. Six weeks ago.'

'That's past the usual incubation time for malaria...' Tim had clearly divined the direction that Megan was moving in, and waved his hand towards Jaye. 'Ask my friend over there. He's a doctor.'

'You've taken two of these?' Jaye held the blister pack up. The log in the medicine cabinet had indicated a full box of paracetamol and there were two missing from the blister pack.

'That was a while ago...'

Tim reached for the blister pack, and Megan caught his hand. 'You don't need any more, Tim. Just sit quietly.'

'You think it might be malaria?' Jaye murmured.

Megan reddened, as if she'd been caught doing something she shouldn't, turning her gaze up towards him. 'I didn't say that.'

Jaye supposed that, as the doctor in attendance, he ought to take over now. But Megan was doing fine on her own—a lot better than fine. She'd thought to take the paracetamol away from Tim before he took another dose, and her firm but gentle way seemed to be working with his friend, who was notoriously unwilling to do anything the doctor told him.

'You know what to look for.' He stepped back, motioning for Megan to carry on with her examination.

Megan nodded, laying her hand on Tim's chest. 'You have a bit of a wheeze there. When did you say this started?'

'Tuesday...no, Wednesday. I was over it by Thursday lunchtime.'

'Three days ago.' Megan seemed to realise that the best way to get Tim to co-operate was to tell him exactly what was going on.

'I've been home for six weeks...nearly seven.' Tim started to shiver. He was obviously feeling very ill, and his tone was probably sharper than he'd meant it to be. But Megan didn't waver.

'*Plasmodium Malariae* can take up to forty-nine days to incubate and has different symptoms from the other types of malaria.' She glanced up at Jaye and he nodded. 'I think we might look at it as a possibility. Particularly as you may have some level of immunity from the amount of time you're spent in regions where it's endemic.'

She reached for the throw that was draped across the back of the chair and tucked it around Tim. Just the right mixture of care and cajoling.

'Yeah. S'pose so…'

'In which case we should get you a blood test as soon as possible, then we'll know for sure. If it's flu, I'll be happy for you to say that you told me so.'

'And if it's malaria, you'll tell me you told me so.' Tim managed a smile.

'I'll forgo that pleasure, on condition you take the drugs to get it cleared up.'

Tim nodded. 'Perhaps the doctor will make himself useful and give us a lift.'

Megan reddened again. 'We should see what Jaye thinks…' Her gaze found Jaye, a look of clear apology on her face.

That wasn't needed. Megan had done exactly the right thing, and she'd charmed Tim into facing the possibilities that he must have already been aware of.

'I'll go and get my bag. And call my father.'

Tim groaned. 'Oh, please. Surely we don't need any more reinforcements, do we? People get malaria all the time…'

Jaye chuckled, turning away. He imagined that Megan could handle Tim while he was gone.

* * *

It was extraordinary. Five years ago, when she'd seen him at the hospital, Jaye had hardly seemed to notice anyone as lowly as a nurse. But now he was allowing her to take charge and examine his friend.

He must have a reason to act so completely out of character. Then the idea occurred to Megan that maybe he wasn't acting out of character, that she'd been wrong about him all along. That was a little too delicious to contemplate right now.

'It's probably best to go to Gloucester Central.' Raj had checked Megan's observations and was writing a referral note for the hospital. 'They have the facilities for out-of-hours testing, so they can get the blood test done tomorrow.'

He tore the sheet from his pad and handed it to Megan. 'Make sure the doctor gets this, won't you? I don't want him listening to Tim and sending him home with a flu diagnosis.'

'Doctors…' Tim muttered under his breath. His cheeks were flushed with fever and he was grumbling quietly. 'Give me a nurse any day.'

'My sentiments entirely.' Jaye shot Megan a grin that made her stomach turn somersaults, and then twitched at the throw that covered Tim's legs. Tim protested, grabbing it tightly.

'Come on. Let's get you to the car.'

Megan had given Raj's letter to the doctor at the hospital, who had read the few paragraphs in instalments, stopping every now and then to turn his attention somewhere else.

'Dr Perera has extensive experience with tropical diseases.' She tapped her finger on the top of the letter to draw the doctor's attention back from the Saturday evening bustle that was going on around them, and Jaye allowed himself to smile. She was unshakeable.

'In that case… I assume the patient's been abroad?'

'Yes, six weeks ago. As you'll see from Dr Perera's letter.'

'Yes, of course.' The doctor gave up the unequal struggle and focussed entirely on Megan for a moment. 'I agree that admitting him for tests would be wise. You're his wife?'

The doctor could be forgiven for thinking that. It had taken Megan just an hour or so to build up the kind of trust with Tim that looked as if they'd known each other for years.

'No. His partner is on his way.' Megan had dealt with that, too. She'd countered Tim's protests with the observation that if it were *her* partner on his way to hospital, there would be hell to pay afterwards if she hadn't received a call. Tim had acquiesced and had asked Jaye to call David.

'Okay… Good. Next of kin?'

'Oh, for goodness' sake. I'm hardly going to die…' Tim roused himself from the doze he'd fallen into and Megan turned towards him.

'Red tape. You know all about that, don't you?' Her smile placated Tim and his head fell back onto the pillow.

'David Foreman. Same address as the patient.' Jaye supplied the necessary information, and the doctor hurried away.

'Don't work for this guy. Come and work for me, I need a nurse.' Tim reached for Megan's hand.

'You do not.' Indignation flashed through Jaye.

'It's tempting…' Megan paused for a moment, clearly pretending to think about it. 'But I'm very happy with the job I have. And my current employer.'

That was a turn-up for the books. If the last four days had accomplished nothing else, it seemed that Megan was finally beginning to trust him. Jaye hid his elation, throwing his friend an amused glare.

'You heard the lady. Just rest, will you.'

'Hmm. Thought I'd give it a try.' Tim moved fitfully on the bed, obviously uncomfortable, and then his hand flew to his mouth. Somehow Megan managed to find a cardboard dish and hold it in front of him before he started to vomit.

Jaye had wondered whether Megan would want to leave now, but she insisted they stay until David arrived. Tim's partner walked into the cubicle half an hour later, in a state of barely concealed panic.

'What's he been up to now?'

'It could be nothing. Just a nasty dose of flu.' Jaye stayed silent, and Megan answered.

'Okay, you've given me the good news…'

Megan smiled. 'The bad news isn't that bad. It could be malaria and the hospital's going to run some tests tomorrow.'

'Malaria?' David puffed out a breath, running his hand across the top of his head. 'Can they treat that? I'm an English teacher, all I know about malaria is from Victorian novels.'

'Medicine's come a long way since then. If the tests show that Tim does have malaria, the doctors will be able to tell you what type and offer the relevant treatment.'

'Right. Thanks.' David sat down by the side of the bed. 'What do I need to do now?'

'Just be with him. The porters will be along in a moment to take him up to the ward. He's being well looked after, and he'll be feeling much better soon. Make sure he does what he's told, though.'

'Oh, yes. He's going to do exactly as he's told.' David looked up at Jaye. 'Thanks for picking this up. I thought he just had flu. I never would have imagined it might be malaria.'

'You have Megan to thank for that. I just drove.'

Again, that look of embarrassed apology flashed across Megan's face. David turned to her and she smiled at him.

'Thank you, Megan, I appreciate it. I dare say that Tim will when he's feeling a bit better.' David knew better than anyone that Tim could be stubborn.

'He's been a model patient.' Megan grinned and David smiled suddenly.

'Yeah. I believe that one…'

They waited until the porter arrived to take Tim up to the ward, and then David insisted they leave. They walked towards Jaye's car together, Megan bundled in the thick dark blue fleece that his father had grabbed from the pile of coats that hung on the back of the kitchen door. Now that he had time to think about it, Jaye realised that it was his.

It was oddly exciting, and he caught his breath as she put her hands in the pockets, wondering if she knew. She seemed lost in thought, and the impulse to put his arm around her was almost overwhelming.

'You meant what you said? About being very happy with your job…?' He left out the part about being happy with her employer, too. That could refer to the charity as a whole and wasn't necessarily personal, although it had felt very personal at the time.

'Yes, I did.' Megan looked up at him. 'Anyway, Tim has a temperature of a hundred and two.'

'Just checking.' Jaye opened the car door for her. 'I wouldn't stand in your way if you decided that we weren't right for you.'

'Really? I'm disappointed.' She shot him a wry smile as she climbed into the car.

'Okay, so I'd fight tooth and nail. But I thought it was

only fair to mention it.' Jaye closed the car door before Megan could change her mind.

'I'd like to check something too.' She spoke as soon as he got into the driver's seat. 'I didn't mean to suggest a diagnosis... You're the doctor.'

If that was all she was worried about then she could stop now. 'I'm glad you did. You were ahead of me in thinking about the possibility of malaria.'

Megan laughed suddenly. 'That was actually a misinterpretation on my part. When I found David down in the kitchen, it occurred to me that you and he had dreamed up one last test for us all.'

'We wouldn't have done that. It's a party, not a challenge.'

'And it wouldn't have been a very good challenge, hiding himself away down in the kitchen, where no one was likely to find him. Then I realised he was burning up and that he was really ill, but not before an entire list of tropical diseases had flashed through my mind.'

'Well, I dare say we would have worked our way around to it, but you saved some time.' Jaye turned the key in the ignition and the engine purred into life. 'I don't suppose you fancy a nightcap since we've missed the party now?'

She nodded almost immediately. 'Yes, thank you. That would be very nice.'

CHAPTER FIVE

MEGAN WAS ONE of a kind. Capable and firm, and yet she saw what other people needed and responded to that. Honest to a fault, but her warmth and wry smile took the sharp edges from her observations.

And if he hadn't met a woman like her before, then maybe the rules he'd set himself didn't apply. Jaye decided to think about that when he wasn't so intoxicated with her scent.

The lights were out in the main part of the house, and he drove to the west side, stopping the car on the hard standing outside his apartment. Megan got out of the car, and he switched on the light in the porch so she could see her way.

She was looking around, always interested in the things around her. 'What's this…?' Her gaze was fixed on the doorframe. 'A mouse!'

'That's Henry.' Jaye smiled. He'd named the tiny carved mouse when he'd been a boy, and this side of the house was closed up. Now it welcomed him home every time he stepped through the front door, but suddenly it felt as if he was seeing it for the first time again.

'Henry the mouse.' She bent to get a better view of him, running her fingers over the wood, smoothed and hardened by time. 'Hello, Henry. What have you seen, in all the years you've been here?'

'Quite a few things, I imagine…' Jaye opened the door and ushered her inside. 'This is the oldest part of the house. It dates back to Tudor times.'

'It doesn't seem…' Megan turned around full circle, looking at the wooden staircase and the gallery running around the top storey of the hallway. 'It's much lighter than I'd have imagined. I always think of Tudor houses as very small and cramped.'

'This was the entrance to the old manor house. It was designed to make an impression.' Megan looked and commented on things, just as most other people did, but Jaye didn't mind that. She somehow didn't make him feel that he was an insignificant part of a greater whole.

'Well, it works. I'm impressed.' She turned to him, and it seemed that the world lurched under his feet. As if he were about to trip and fall right into her beautiful blue eyes.

He tore himself away from that precipice, taking her coat and hanging it up, allowing himself just a moment to appreciate her scent before he withdrew from that dizzying experience.

'Would you like some cocoa, or something a bit stronger? Or a guided tour…?' Jaye could take or leave the first two options, but badly wanted Megan to choose the third.

'Cocoa would be nice. *And* the guided tour?'

Jaye turned away from her, hiding his smile, and led her through to the kitchen. While he heated the milk, Megan gave his kitchen a thorough once-over.

'The kitchen's newly built?' She ran her hand across the worktop. The fact that she seemed unable to look without touching sent a shiver down Jaye's spine.

'Yes, I had the extension built when I took over this wing as my own apartment. I wanted something modern, but didn't want to change what was already here.'

'You dug these foundations?' There was a trace of mischief in her smile.

'No. I'm to be trusted with a spade but not a mechanical digger.' Jaye suddenly wished that he had, if it would make him any more acceptable in Megan's eyes. If it would chase away the feeling that his own privilege was exactly the kind of thing that her father had offered, and she had rejected.

She nodded. 'Probably wise. You'd have been sorry if you'd knocked a few walls down by mistake.'

'Yes, I would. I'm supposed to be a caretaker here.'

'For future generations?'

'For whatever comes next.' Jaye didn't think a lot about future generations, and if he did it was his brothers' children, not his own.

He made the cocoa and then took her upstairs to the gallery, the old floorboards creaking under their feet. She leaned over the bannister, looking down, and wondered aloud whether fine ladies had done the same, to inspect the tops of young men's heads for bald patches. In the spare bedroom she exclaimed at the four-poster bed, and downstairs in the living room she turned the corners of her mouth down when she found that the flowers in the old brick fireplace weren't real.

'They last longer...' Jaye hadn't really thought about it before.

'But they have no scent.'

Next time he'd make sure that there was a vase full of fresh-picked flowers there. Jaye made the resolution, despite the fact that *next time* wasn't all that likely.

But Megan had moved on. 'The windows... Some of this is new glass and some old?'

Jaye joined her at the mullioned window. Looking into the darkness beyond, feeling the cold under his fingertips as he touched the glass, gave him an odd feeling of craving. To see what she saw, and feel what she felt.

'I wanted to save as much of the old glass as I could, but some of the pieces were too badly damaged. So, rather than try to reproduce them, I replaced them with new glass.'

'Arrested decay?' Megan immediately got what he'd been trying to do and Jaye smiled. 'I like that. It's honest.'

'In a place this old you either have to strip everything out and start again, or you have to live with the irregularities.' Jaye liked the irregularities.

She nodded, looking up at him. Her face was pale in the moonlight, her eyes wide. Jaye wondered whether she would object if he asked whether he could kiss her.

Or maybe he should just do it. She seemed closer now, and that definitely wasn't a trick of the light. He was surrounded by her scent, and could almost feel the warmth of her body against his.

'Oh…' She gave him a startled look, and Jaye instinctively moved back. Her hand flew to her wrist. 'My bangle. I think I've lost it.'

He brushed away the impulse to tell her that the bangle didn't matter, and that he'd buy her as many new ones as she wanted, if she'd only stay in this moment with him. The look of dismay on Megan's face told him that the bangle *did* matter.

'I'm sorry… It's really precious to me. It was given to me by the people I worked with when I left Africa.'

'Do you remember where you last had it?' This wasn't just a chunk of silver, it was suddenly as important to Jaye as it obviously was to Megan.

'I…' She thought for a moment. 'I took it off when I was with Tim in the snug… I didn't want to examine him while I was wearing heavy jewellery.'

'And you left it there?'

'I think so. I must have done.' She shrugged, trying to cover her dismay. 'I dare say it'll be safe enough. I can go and look for it first thing in the morning.'

'There's no point in worrying about it all night. We'll go and find it now.'

Megan hurried towards the front door of his apartment, apparently quite prepared to go out into the night wearing just her dress if it meant she might find the bangle. Jaye turned her around, taking her hand and leading her to the back of the entrance hall.

'This is a bit quicker.' He grinned at her, unlocking the door that led to the narrow servants' corridor and ushering her through to the concealed door at the other end, which opened into the main part of house.

'You'd hardly know this was there.' She ran her fingers along the mouldings that disguised the door.

Jaye nodded. 'It's how the servants used to appear out of nowhere and then disappear again. But it's the best way of getting around the house.'

'Do you have lots of secret passages like this?'

'A few.' He led her downstairs to the kitchen, flipping on the light.

Megan hurried through to where Tim had been sitting, looking under the table while Jaye moved the chairs. Then she got down on her hands and knees to scan the floor. 'There it is. Look, under the sideboard.'

She tried to reach under the heavy piece of furniture, and frowned in exasperation, hitching her dress up a little to give herself more freedom of movement. Jaye moved her to one side, feeling a moment's regret as her hemline slipped back down to her knees, and reached under the sideboard.

His fingers touched the bangle, and it rolled a little to one side. He reached a little further, and got hold of it.

'Thank you.' Her face was shining as he put it over her hand, back onto her wrist. 'I don't think I could have gone to sleep not knowing whether I'd lost it.'

The last thing that Jaye wanted to do right now was sleep. He wanted to kiss her, but that probably wasn't anywhere on the agenda that Megan seemed to have planned so carefully for her life. *He* wasn't anywhere on that agenda.

'Is there another secret passage? That'll take us back?'

She'd already seen the one that ran back to his apartment. But her bright excitement made Jaye feel like a boy again. A boy who knew every inch of this house, and who had often left his bed in the middle of the night to explore it when his friends came to stay. A boy who hadn't been afraid of the reaction it might provoke, and who had just enjoyed sharing the excitement of the house's secrets.

'You want secret passages?' He gazed into her shining eyes. 'Your wish is my command, milady. Maybe not in those shoes, though.'

He rummaged in the cupboard under the stairs, and apologised when he could only find a pair of wellingtons. Megan's fingers trembled as she pulled them on. Secret passages. A handsome man to show her through them. She couldn't help hoping for shadows and a little darkness, too.

She wanted to go with him, into the shadows, even though she couldn't see what lay ahead. Even though there could be no plan, no carefully thought-out assessment of cause and effect. The man she'd thought she'd known had been slowly chipped away this evening, and all she could see now was the boy who had named a tiny carved mouse. The one who'd climbed through windows and skinned his knees. The one who'd looked up at the paintings of his ancestors, knowing that his whole life was in front of him, and that he could be whatever he wanted to be.

'Are you sure?' She nodded down at the wellingtons. They fitted, but looked a little odd with her dress.

'The passage runs under the house, and the floor's pretty uneven and sometimes a bit wet. You'll ruin your shoes.' Jaye grinned. 'Anyway, this is a midnight adventure. It's a come-as-you-are thing. Did I tell you that you looked absolutely gorgeous tonight?'

'No. You didn't.' She'd been so busy avoiding him that Jaye wouldn't have had the chance. 'I feel a bit rumpled now.'

'But still gorgeous.' He caught her hand, leading her past the kitchen and down another narrow flight of steps to the wine cellar. Megan was losing her bearings, but this must be the older part of the house, under Jaye's apartment.

He stopped beside a metal grille, and Megan shivered as cool air brushed her face. Before she could tell him that she didn't need it, he'd taken his jacket off, draping it around her shoulders.

Bending to open one of the cardboard boxes stacked against the wall, he took out two candles, handing her one and lighting it. He swung the grille open and Megan peered into the gloom.

'Where does this go? Is it an escape route?'

Jaye chuckled. 'Yes, it comes up in the old stables. Apparently the fourth Duke had a habit of making this way out to the stables every time his debtors came knocking on the door. And the story is that the seventh Duke would smuggle his lover in through here. Not very convenient for the poor woman, I imagine.'

He held out his arm, and Megan slipped her hands into the sleeves of his jacket, pulling them up over her wrists so she could cling to him. Jaye was sure-footed in the half-light and obviously knew this tunnel well.

'So what number are you?' The Dukes of Marlowe seemed to go back a very long way.

'My uncle was seventeen. Which makes me eighteen.'

'Not your mother…?' Megan had wondered how Jaye had inherited the title when his parents were both still alive.

'No. My uncle had no children and I was the oldest male heir. It's an old-fashioned system that doesn't allow women to inherit. I'm hoping that'll change for the next generation.'

'And the house came with the title?'

'Yes, the house and land are entailed. Although my parents have always run the estate. It suits us all and gives me the opportunity to spend more time with the charity.'

'Then you don't spend much time here?'

'Not in the last few years. I haven't been in this tunnel in a while. When I was a boy, and my friends stayed over, we used to creep down here at night all the time.'

So this was an escape for him, too. Megan imagined that the tunnel had been waiting, silent and dark beneath the house, for the moment when Jaye returned.

'It's wonderful. Every house should have one.'

'I think so, too.' Jaye stopped suddenly. Then she felt the brush of his fingers, as gentle on the side of her face as the cool breeze that ventilated the tunnel. Then his lips, leaving just the ghost of a kiss on her forehead.

'It's a tradition.' Megan shivered as his breath caressed her ear. 'No Duke of Marlowe can bring a woman down here without kissing her.'

'Then it would be a shame if you fell short of your duties.'

'My thoughts exactly. Particularly as I've never had the chance to fulfil this particular one before.'

Megan caught her breath. Suddenly it seemed important that she wasn't just treading the same path that other women had taken, that this was something different, and that it was hers alone.

'As it's your first time, I'll have to forgive you for taking half-measures.'

'Half-measures?' There was something suddenly taut about the feel of his body next to hers. Something deliciously compelling about the tone of his voice.

He took the candle from her, propping it next to his own on a ledge that ran along the side of the wall. She caught a tantalising glimpse of his smile in the flickering light as the candle flared and guttered.

Jaye's arm steadied her. And then she was *in* his arms. She felt his lips against hers and almost cried out. He kissed her again, and this time it was like liquid fire running through her veins, making her knees shake.

'You fulfil your duties very well, my lord.'

'I find it deliciously easy, my lady…' The pressure of his arm around her waist loosened. There *was* a way back if she chose to take it. But Megan didn't want to.

They were just play-acting, weren't they? Fooling around in a secret tunnel, like he had when he'd been a child.

But his blood was thundering through his veins. And the last time he'd been down here, fooling around, had merely consisted of lighting a few candles and sharing a chocolate bar with his friends, then creeping back to his bed, his pyjamas flapping wetly around his ankles.

When he let Megan go, she grabbed his shirt, pulling him back close. As his body touched hers, she gave a little sigh.

'Jaye…'

When she whispered his name, it was an expression of the need that he felt too. And he needed so badly to touch her skin.

Jaye pulled the neck of his jacket to one side, wondering whether she'd stop him. As he ran his fingers across the bare skin of her neck, she gasped, stretching up against him for another kiss. Blindly, lost in a passion that robbed him of every restraint, he slid the jacket off her shoulders and down to her elbows.

She let out a gasp of approval as he bunched the fabric between his fingers, pinning her arms loosely at her sides and brushing his lips against her forehead.

'That's good. Jaye…'

He couldn't resist. Imprisoning her tightly, he kissed her again. Megan's response was immediate, kissing him back with an almost savage passion that left him reeling.

As soon as he released his grip, she put her arms around his neck, pulling him down for another kiss. He held her tightly against his chest, wondering what he could ever have done to deserve this second chance.

'This… It's not right…' Megan deserved more than this dank, draughty tunnel. She deserved candlelight and soft sheets. Maybe a hot bath, to make her feel good, before he made love to her.

He could hardly breathe. Asking her back to his bed seemed like the biggest risk he'd ever taken.

'No, it's not…' He felt her body pulling slowly away from his. 'You're my boss and…it's too complicated.'

That wasn't what he'd meant. But suddenly it seemed undeniably true. He pulled his jacket up around her shoulders, wrapping it around her.

He'd thought that Megan was so different. She'd seen past the privilege of his background, and that had blinded him to the one thing that was staring him right in the face. He was her boss, and she couldn't see past that. She never would, her father had seen to that.

And this was no misunderstanding. It wasn't right for either of them.

Jaye took her hand, brushing his lips against the backs of her fingers. 'I'll take you back. Tonight never happened.'

'Thank you.' Her eyes glistened as she looked up at him. 'I'm sorry that…it couldn't.'

So was Jaye. But he was beginning to feel as if he'd had a lucky escape.

He took her hand, leading her back out of the tunnel and through the basement to the kitchen. She took off the wellington books, stowing them carefully back into the cupboard under the stairs and slipping her shoes back on. Then she took his jacket off, carefully hanging it over the back of one of the chairs around the kitchen table, her hand smoothing the creases he'd made when he'd pulled her close and kissed her.

'I can find my way from here.' Clearly she didn't want the indignity of being spotted with her boss at one in the morning. Anger surged through Jaye's heart. Why couldn't she see that he was different from her father?

'I'll see you in the morning.' His words were a little more abrupt than he'd meant them to be and he struggled to smile at her. This *was* for the best, and the least he could do was be civil about it. 'Goodnight. Sleep well.'

'Thank you. You too.' Megan turned and walked away from him.

Megan didn't dare to go down to breakfast, making do with an oat bar she'd found at the bottom of her handbag and a glass of water. She packed her things, and sat down to write a note.

Everyone was leaving this morning, and she wondered whether it would be more inconspicuous to go with a group of the others or to walk across the entrance hall alone. Deciding that going it alone had the advantage of allowing her to make a dash for it, she crept downstairs into the quiet entrance hall.

'Not again.' She'd positioned the envelope, addressed to Caroline, next to the flowers on the hall table, when Jaye's voice rang out. Megan jumped, letting out an involuntary yelp of surprise.

'I'm sorry. I didn't see you.' He was sitting in an' armchair right at the back of the entrance hall, behind the stairs.

'I imagine if you had, you'd be leaving by the back door right now.' His voice was kind, but his eyes were devoid of any emotion. The Jaye she'd got a glimpse of last night was lost behind the façade of a charming host.

'I had to come this way, to leave a thank-you note for your mother.' Megan picked up the envelope from the hall table.

'That's very thoughtful. I'll give it to her.'

Megan hesitated. They were both thinking it, so she may as well say it. 'So I'm not so much sneaking off as... leaving unobtrusively.'

'That makes all the difference.' For a moment she thought she saw Jaye's warmth in the flash of his dark eyes.

She held out her hand to him, and he took it, his fingers squeezing hers slightly before he let go again. 'Thank you very much. The last four days have been... It was a really good course.'

If he'd decided to withdraw the job offer after last night, he gave no hint of it. But Jaye was like her father, able to give or take away on a whim, without needing to explain himself.

'Good luck. I'm really looking forward to hearing how you do in Sri Lanka. I hope we meet again on your return.'

He was speaking in code, but it was one that was easily cracked. Her job was safe, and she was still going to

Sri Lanka. And he wasn't going to do anything crazy, like turn up out of the blue while she was there.

'Thank you Jaye. I really appreciate that.'

He nodded. 'May I walk you to your car?'

'Thank you. That would be nice.'

He lifted her suitcase into the boot for her and stood back, watching as she drove away. As the drive wound away from the house, and he disappeared from view, it was impossible not to feel a sense of relief, mixed with sadness. In the hothouse atmosphere of the last four days, Megan had experienced almost every emotion, most of them connected with Jaye in some way.

They'd done the right thing, though, in keeping things simple. When they saw each other next, they would both have forgotten all about what might so easily have happened, but hadn't.

And in the meantime… Sri Lanka beckoned, like a golden glow on the horizon.

CHAPTER SIX

*Two months later. Rural airstrip, Western Province,
Sri Lanka.*

JAYE HAD PUT all his efforts into getting the precious medical supplies out of the plane's cargo hold and stacked by the
side of the tarmac. The pilot had made it very clear that the
only thing he did between landing and taking off again was
to drink iced tea and sit in the shade, and the helpers he'd
been promised by the clinic hadn't turned up yet.

It didn't matter. He'd been sitting down for too long,
first on the flight from Heathrow and then in the cramped
cockpit of the chartered cargo plane, and it had given him
far too long to think about this. A little hard work was more
than welcome.

Something was wrong at the clinic. They were short-
staffed, having lost a couple of nurses and the doctor in
residence in the last month, and Ranjini, the head of nursing
services, had reported that morale was very low. Then, out
of the blue, Megan had put in an urgent request for medical supplies that they should already have.

Jaye had become increasingly worried. When he'd last
spoken with Ranjini, he'd asked her what she needed him
to do and she'd answered straight away.

We cannot work this out on the phone. I need you here, Jaye.

There had been no time to contact Megan, and if there had been Jaye wasn't sure what he would have said. That one kiss had echoed in his memory, along with the promise to himself that it wouldn't be repeated, and together they'd morphed into a longing that he didn't know how to handle.

He'd packed his bags and left, hitching a ride with the medical shipment for the last leg of his journey. Ranjini wouldn't have called him there unless there were serious problems, and getting to the bottom of them was more important than his own feelings, or Megan's for that matter.

He heard an engine, and stood up, stretching his back. A battered motorbike was speeding towards the plane, kicking up dust on the dirt airstrip. For the first time in the last three days Jaye smiled. No one kicked dust up quite as well as Dinesh.

Someone was on the back of the bike, but since they were travelling at speed and seemed to be wearing the better half of the road, it was difficult to make out who it was. But when the passenger dismounted, he recognised Megan even before she'd taken off her helmet, shaking her blonde hair in the breeze.

Even now, the familiar pain twisted in his heart. How often in the last two months had he longed for just a glimpse of her? Just one touch of her fingertips.

He watched as Dinesh took a brush from under the seat and flicked it across his beloved machine. Jaye never had got to the bottom of why he rode through every dust bowl and puddle he came across when he was so very particular about the motorbike being spotless when it was stationary. Perhaps he just liked cleaning it.

Megan had turned towards him, shading her eyes against the sun, and suddenly stood stock-still. Jaye began to walk towards her, and she seemed to gather her wits, hurrying in his direction.

He'd run through this moment so many times in his mind. He was here to solve problems, to be an arbiter if one was needed, and that meant that he had to swallow his own feelings and treat Megan exactly the same as he treated everyone else.

Still, all he could see was her hair, shining in the sunlight. All he could think about was her smile, and how her dusty clothes only served to make her cheeks look pinker and her eyes even more lustrously blue. Despite everything, he still ached to kiss her.

Which was impossible on just about every level imaginable. Megan didn't want it, she'd made that pretty clear. And Jaye still had a little bit of his pride intact.

'Jaye…' He'd known it would be hard, but he hadn't quite anticipated how hard it would be to hear her say his name. 'What are you doing here? I thought the relief doctor—'

'Dr Stone won't be able to fly out until next week. I'm filling in for him. Didn't Ranjini tell you?'

'No…no, we've been very busy. She left me a note saying that a doctor was coming with the medical supplies and I thought it would be Dr Stone. I came to meet you because…'

Suddenly, a tear dropped from her eye. Megan wiped it away impatiently, leaving a smear of grime on her cheek.

'What's the matter?' Jaye fisted his hands at his sides to stop himself from holding out his arms, ready to comfort her.

'It's nothing.' She shook her head to emphasise the point. It was the death knell to all the vain hopes that had intruded into his waking and sleeping for the last two months. Even when she was angry with him, Megan had always told him why.

'I mean…yes, there's something the matter. We have a boy with dengue fever at the clinic. I need you to go to him. Dinesh will take you.'

'Okay.' It was almost a relief to think about something else. 'What's his condition?'

'He's starting to haemorrhage. We're desperately low on IV fluids. Have you brought some with the supplies?'

Jaye had just unloaded the box, and he started to walk towards it. 'Over here. You have no IV fluids?'

'I'll explain later. You should go.'

Jaye tore open the box with rather more force than necessary. Something was going on, and it looked as if Megan was as likely to tell him as fly in the air. If she wanted him to just be her boss, he'd *be* her boss, and that meant she had some questions to answer.

Megan watched as Jaye drove Dinesh's bike away from the airstrip, followed by the obligatory plume of dust. The horror when she'd first seen Jaye had given way to a sudden joy, a feeling that everything was going to be all right. Which was even more terrifying.

Dinesh had handed his bike over to Jaye with little more than a murmur. The people here trusted him. It was good that he'd come because the clinic needed a firm hand to steer it right now. If that hand happened to be Jaye's then there was no reason for Megan to start fantasising about all the other things that he could do with his hands.

And she didn't have time for that, anyway. The truck from the clinic would be here soon and there were medical supplies to load. She'd survived the four days of Jaye's presence and two months of his absence. She could manage to get through the next week until the new doctor arrived.

An hour later, she navigated the bumpy track that led to the clinic, brick built and shaded by trees that seemed even more lush and inviting after the heat of the road. Her arms ached from lifting boxes and the heavy steering on the truck, and Megan was glad to be back, even if it did bring her in closer proximity to Jaye.

Dinesh jumped down from the passenger seat, making for his bike, clearly intent on giving it a thorough once-over and applying a little man-to-bike reassurance that allowing someone else to take charge of it had been an exception to the rule and wouldn't be happening again. Megan felt suddenly too weary to move.

A tap on the door made her jump, and as she opened it Ranjini stood back so that the shower of dust didn't spoil the bright colours of her sari. 'Jaye's here?'

Ranjini gave her usual broad smile. 'Yes. He has seen to the boy and is making a round of all the patients now.'

'How is Ashan?'

'We have what we need for him. He will be well now.'

'Good. Did Jaye say anything…?' Megan hardly dared ask. But asking Ranjini was a good deal easier than approaching Jaye. 'Did he want to see me?'

'When he has finished his rounds. You have plenty of time to go and get cleaned up, he is taking his time.' Ranjini leaned forward, laying her hand on Megan's arm. 'He is here now. Things will be better, you'll see.'

'I hope so.'

'You do not know him as we do.'

Megan felt a tear prick at the side of her eye. This time she managed to blink it back.

'You are very tired.' Ranjini was looking at her, concern in her face.

'We all are. But things will get better. I'm just going to count the boxes off the truck, and then I'll go and have a shower.'

In the shower, her tears would be unnoticeable, even to

herself. She'd towel herself dry and pretend that everything was all right. Pretend that she didn't want to see Jaye's smile because, now more than ever, it was impossible.

Triple-checking each box off the lorry and into the stock-room took longer than Megan had thought. By the time she'd cleaned up and changed her clothes, the word around the clinic was that Jaye was waiting for her in the office that Dr Clarke had recently vacated.

He'd tidied up a bit, putting all the papers that had been left scattered across the desk into a neat pile. A new pile of patients' case notes had appeared and he was obviously working his way through it, a cup of tea at his elbow. When Megan appeared in the open doorway he looked up.

'Come in, Megan. Shut the door.'

A chair was positioned on the other side of the desk, and the tray that was on the desk contained an extra cup and saucer. Jaye had obviously prepared for this interview, and Megan still felt completely unprepared.

'Would you like some tea?'

'No. Thank you.' The pouring of tea was only going to prolong this agony. 'You want to know why we ran out of essential drugs for the clinic.'

'Yes. I'd very much like to know that.' His face was impassive. Maybe he felt nothing. It had only been one kiss and he could be forgiven for that.

'When I first arrived here, I did a thorough stock check. I sent a copy through to the London office.'

He nodded. 'Yes, I looked that up when I saw your emergency requisition. It indicates that you had good stock levels.'

'We thought we did. But one of the nurses came to me with a batch of medicines that had a current date on the outer box, but the packs inside were out of date. I investigated a bit more, and found a lot more like that in the stockroom. There were dressings that were covered with mould as well.'

Jaye's brow was furrowed. 'You're saying that our suppliers are sending you old stock?'

'No, because I looked up the records, and some of those boxes had been opened and checked before, and they were fine.'

'So…?' His gaze suddenly met hers. Searching, as if he wanted to turn over the darkest recesses of her mind. He'd done that when he'd kissed her, and she'd revelled in the way he'd seemed to want to gauge her every response. But now it felt like a searing condemnation.

'So someone here has taken the new supplies from the boxes and replaced them with old ones. Probably drugs that have been marked out of date and put to one side to be destroyed.'

'You're saying that we have a thief. Working here in the clinic?'

'I don't know.' Megan felt suddenly angry. Jaye was probing her but giving nothing back. She didn't want any special consideration from him, but she'd bet her life he didn't treat the rest of the clinic staff like this.

'Make a guess.' There was no humour in his face as he said the words.

'Okay… On the same day this all came to light, one of the nurses left early, saying she was ill. She hasn't been back here since and we've gone to her house and she isn't there. She's worked here a while and she was good at her job. I have no evidence against her, but it's a coincidence.'

'All right.' He picked up his pen and started to scribble notes on the pad in front of him. 'I'll take it from here. Anything else?'

Yes, there was a lot else. The bad feeling in the clinic, the way that Dr Clarke had acted. The fact that this job wasn't what anyone had promised, and now Jaye was here and treating her like the person he least wanted to see.

Okay. She hadn't much wanted to see him either. But at least she was trying.

'I'm doing a thorough stock check. I'll know exactly how much we have of everything, and have the old stock ready for disposal in a couple of days.'

'I want to see all the stock before you destroy anything. And your stock check, please.' Jaye didn't look up at her.

'All right.' Perhaps she should go now. But it felt as if there was nothing but unfinished business here. 'Is there anything else?'

For a moment his eyes softened. She saw the man she'd opened her heart to over that turbulent four days.

'Yes.'

Megan nodded, waiting for him to elaborate. Then the Jaye she knew seemed to snap back out of focus, retreating into cool professionalism. The man who had seemed to understand everything now appeared intent on understanding nothing.

'Ranjini and Dr Narayan ran this place for a long time together, almost since it started. They made a reality of our original vision, that it would be a calm and quiet place of healing.'

He said the words almost as if he'd never said them before. Almost as if they'd never met before.

'Yes. I know.'

'When Dr Narayan retired, and we replaced him with Dr Clarke…well, you knew that there were some teething problems before you came here.'

Teething problems. That was one way of putting it. 'Dr Clarke had a very confrontational approach. A lot of the staff are unhappy and claim they've been treated unfairly. I know that Ranjini's mentioned this to you.'

'Yes, she has. She tells me that since Dr Clarke left, two weeks ago, you and she have been working very hard. You've been cleaning the wards and filling in for absentee nurses, and now I hear that you've been spending quite a bit of time in the stockroom as well.'

'Yes...' Megan could feel that Jaye was working around to some kind of point. 'The staff shortage...'

'Yes, I understand that. What I don't understand is why I didn't hear about this from you. This isn't the job you were employed to do, and I suspect that neither of us are particularly happy about that. I'm certainly not.'

Something thudded in Megan's chest. Perhaps it was her heart, reacting to the blow that Jaye's ice-cold words had dealt.

'I...' She felt her ears burn. 'I...had some initial concerns, which I spoke with John Ferris about. The first two weeks that I was here I was trying to get the measure of the place, both organisationally and in terms of the personalities involved.'

'And afterwards?'

'John's been away sick for the last two weeks.'

'Yes, I know. I've been filling in for him in London.' Jaye leaned back in his chair, swiping his hand across the top of his head. 'You've clearly been unhappy here, and things are falling apart. I'll ask again. Why didn't you tell me?'

Was he really that obtuse? Or was he just making this more difficult for her, because he knew that he could? Suddenly Megan didn't care that he was her boss, or that it was in his power to send her home if he felt like it. He couldn't treat her like this.

'Why do you think, Jaye?'

CHAPTER SEVEN

'WHY DO YOU THINK?'

That was the one question that Jaye didn't want to answer. He didn't want to say that he'd wondered whether Megan even remembered their kiss, when he'd been able to think about little else.

'It's not a matter of what *I* think. It's a matter of why you didn't report back to me.'

The little tilt of her chin told him that she was done with agreeing with him, and was going to meet him head on. A little thrill of respect fluttered in Jaye's chest.

'Let's not beat about the bush, Jaye. We overstepped the mark, and…there was an inappropriate encounter…'

Inappropriate encounter? He'd called it a lot of things in his own mind, but never that.

'And we let it be.' The thought that Megan hadn't let it be, any more than he had, made Jaye's heart beat a little faster.

'That's just what I was doing. Letting it be. Ranjini was keeping you up to date, and there was no reason for me to call you and say it all over again, particularly when we were so busy.'

'Too busy? You were too busy to call, is that what it is?' Jaye realised he sounded like a petulant teenager.

They were going round in circles here. The elephant in

the room was growing larger by the minute, and threatening to crush them both.

'Look, Megan. I'm not your grandmother, and you don't need to phone for a Sunday afternoon chat every week. But I do need to know if you're unhappy at work.'

'You're the one who said I'm unhappy…'

'Aren't you?'

'Yes, right now I'm very unhappy. Because there are real problems here, and all you can do is swan in and ask me why I didn't call.'

'Because it's a serious point. If you want to work with me, then you have to communicate with me, and if I'm going to be faced with a wall of silence…' She hadn't called because the kiss *had* meant something to her. The thought crashed into Jaye's mind, leaving him trembling from the shock of it.

'Right.' She got to her feet. Jaye was tempted to tell her to sit down because he wasn't finished, but couldn't think of anything else constructive that he wanted to say.

'I'll communicate. Let's see how you handle that, shall we?' She turned, stalking out of the office and banging the door behind her, the glass pane in the top half of it rattling as she did so.

'Good. I'm looking forward to seeing how *you* handle it.' Jaye threw the words after her, although he doubted she'd hear, and slumped back into his chair, his head in his hands.

'That went well.' He chided himself with the thought that he'd completely mismanaged the conversation. From both a professional *and* a personal point of view. He'd had a perfectly good point to make, but he'd craved some kind of reaction and he'd pushed her too hard.

Someone tapped on the door. 'What now?'

He looked up, and saw the bright flash of a sari behind the obscure glass. 'I'm sorry… Come in, Ranjini.'

Ranjini floated into the office, as calm and unflappable as ever. 'I will give your apology back to you since it is directed at the wrong person.'

'You heard?'

'We have had too many raised voices and slammed doors here, Jayananda. I asked you to come, believing you would restore calm.'

Ranjini only called him by his full name when she wanted to reprove him. And right now she had a very good point.

'Yes, I know.' Jaye shook his head, trying to think clearly. 'I'm…pretty jet-lagged. I know that's no excuse and that Megan's tired too. I'm going to apologise.'

Ranjini nodded, as if the apology was all his idea but one she thoroughly approved of. She'd been giving him that nod for nearly thirty years, ever since she'd been a teenager who'd babysat Jaye and his younger brothers when the family had been in Sri Lanka. When he thought about it, his behaviour hadn't improved all that much since then.

'I think that would be a good idea. I wouldn't want to lose Megan, she has been a great gift to us over the last month. She has resolved many difficult issues and worked very hard.'

Guilt throbbed at Jaye's temple. Whatever Megan thought of him, she was a valuable member of staff here. He'd had no right to upset her, however tired and hurt he felt.

'All right. Message received. I'm going to go and eat a large helping of humble pie. You won't lose her.' However angry Megan was, it would pass. And when it did, her commitment to all she could do here would resurface.

'Let her take some time alone. She will reach a point of greater balance. As will you.'

Jaye doubted it. But, then, Ranjini knew both him and

Megan a lot better than they knew each other. Even if it did feel as if they'd looked into each other's souls during those four days they'd spent together.

Ranjini settled back into her chair. 'How are your parents? The last I heard from your mother was that she had a frozen shoulder, but that it was improving?'

'Yes, she's been having physiotherapy and it's much better now.' Ranjini was right in this, too. His own temper was still simmering uncertainly beneath the surface, and he needed to think about something else for a while.

Jaye reached for the bag that he'd dumped by the side of the desk, drawing out the brightly coloured parcel. 'Mum sent this for you. She hopes you like it.'

'Oh! Such pretty paper! What is it?'

'I don't know. And if I did know, I wouldn't tell you. That's the whole point of wrapping it up. Mum wears the scarf you sent her all the time.'

From the size and shape of the package it was another scarf. His mother and Ranjini had been exchanging scarves for years. They were light and easy to send, and always appreciated and worn, which made them an ideal present. But both women still maintained the illusion that they didn't know what was inside the carefully wrapped packages.

'And your brothers? I hear that Caroline is to become a grandmother yet again…'

Jaye leaned back in his chair. By the time he and Ranjini had worked through his brothers and Ranjini's three daughters, he and Megan would both have had every opportunity to cool off. And he would have an apology ready.

'Megan, I said the wrong thing, in the wrong way. I apologise unreservedly.' Jaye's voice behind her sounded stilted and strange.

Megan had retreated to the drugs cupboard to rage a little, cry a little and then tell herself how stupid she'd been. The usual process, which had worked its way inexorably round to the stage of self-reproach and flushes of embarrassment when the slo-mo repeats of what she'd said to Jaye played back in her head.

She took a deep breath, and turned. 'I don't accept your apology.'

His gaze scanned her face. 'You've been crying.'

'Yes. You don't look as if you have.'

That slow smile spread across his face. 'No, I haven't. That doesn't mean I'm not sorry.'

'I don't doubt your sincerity.'

Jaye nodded. 'So you accept the sincerity of my apology, but not the apology itself.'

'You were right. It *was* important that I call you, and I didn't. I was…' Embarrassed. Not sure what Jaye would say. Afraid he might think she was presuming on a relationship they'd both admitted was wrong. Afraid she might break down and cry as soon as she heard his voice….

Megan heaved a sigh. It was too much to go into right now and would only provoke another argument. 'All of the above.'

He shot her a puzzled look, and then smiled, seeming to understand what she meant.

'There was nothing stopping me from picking up the phone either. But…all of the above.'

It was a fragile truce but it could hold. It *had* to hold.

'I'm sorry for slamming your door.'

'Sometimes calm and quiet requires clearing the air first. And I think my door will survive. You didn't hurt it.'

But she'd hurt *him*. If Jaye wanted to pretend that he was only capable of as much feeling as his office door, Megan knew differently. He could retreat behind the mask of good manners, a gentleman in every sense of the word, but she knew that there was a lot more to Jaye than that.

'Look, Jaye, if we're going to work together...'

'You *want* us to work together?' Jaye's smile invaded his eyes suddenly.

'Yes, I want us to work together. Everyone here says that you have an innovative approach and that you're a very good doctor. And a good boss as well. I want to see what you're made of.'

'I want to see what you're made of too.' He was clearly turning his words over carefully in his mind. 'In a professional sense, of course.'

That was a start. And if all that Megan could countenance was a professional relationship, which could bring with it respect and friendship, then that actually was a very great deal.

'There might be a few disagreements along the way.'

'Goes without saying. I wouldn't expect anything less of you, Megan.'

Megan nodded. 'That works for me.'

They stared at each other silently. Jaye was the first to break the spell and suggest a way forward.

'So... Would you like some help with this?'

'You should get some rest. You look tired.'

He nodded. 'Yes, I am. And so are you. But I'm taking a leaf out of your book and mucking in to get things that need doing done.'

'Okay. I have no problem with that.' She picked up the sheaf of papers that contained an entry for every box in the stockroom, ready for the results of the check to be entered. 'Here's what I've done so far.'

Jaye had been prepared to grovel if that was what it took. But Megan had refused to allow him to, and had made it very clear that she wanted more from him than just an apology.

This was what he'd wanted all along, someone to question the things he took for granted, and challenge him. They'd drawn and redrawn the lines and finally this was something that they could both live with. All that he could feel, knowing she wasn't going to give up on him entirely, was a sense of profound relief.

They worked steadily, opening each box and noting down the end dates of every packet of drugs inside. Turn and turn about. Megan called out the dates and Jaye noted them down on the chart, and then they broke for a cup of tea and something to eat. Then he passed the chart over to her and set about opening the next box.

'I think we should call it a day.' It wasn't all that late but fatigue was finally catching up with Jaye, and Megan had suppressed a yawn.

She stood up, slipping the chart in her pocket. 'Okay. I can't actually think of any good reasons to disagree with you on that one.'

'Sure? We could argue about it if you wanted.' The hours of quiet, steady work had slowly dispersed any lingering awkwardness, and the joke seemed like no risk at all.

'Quite sure. I'll get back to you if I reconsider.'

He chuckled. 'Too late. The decision's made now.' He got to his feet, waiting for Megan to follow him out of the stockroom.

She locked the door carefully, checking that it was secure. Then she twisted another key off her key ring, putting it into his hand.

'That's the third key. I have one and Ranjini has the other.'

'So if anything else goes missing we'll know exactly who to blame.'

Megan laughed. 'Yes. You or Ranjini. Because I'll know it isn't me.'

Jaye nodded, trying to hide his smile. He held the door of the main clinic building open for her, drinking in the cool scents of the evening as they stepped outside.

'I always know I'm home when I smell cinnamon bark.'

'Home?' She looked up at him in the darkness.

'This is my second home. England's home too.'

'It must be nice. Having two homes.' There was a trace of sadness in Megan's voice, and Jaye realised he'd never heard her say the word before. She talked about 'her flat' and 'her mother's house', but never home. Perhaps that was one more thing that her father had deprived Megan of. There was nowhere that she felt she had a right to be.

'So where do you call home?'

There was a short silence and then she laughed. 'It's a bit too late in the evening for that kind of question. Right now, home is wherever I can get some sleep.'

Clearly she didn't know where home was, without thinking about it, and his question was a step too far. He'd touched the limit of what Megan was prepared to share with him, and it was time to back off.

'I can identify with needing sleep.' He slowed next to one of the bungalows that housed the staff who lived on site. 'This is me, I think.'

'Goodnight, then.' Megan turned abruptly, clearly determined that he shouldn't walk her to her door. Hurrying to the next bungalow, she opened the door and went inside, not looking back.

He'd watched her to her door instead. So what? That was the very least that could be expected of a man when he'd spent the evening with a woman, even if it had been in a store cupboard. Not ready to sleep just yet, Jaye sat down on the top step of the porch, listening to the night.

* * *

Megan had slept soundly for the first time in a week. And she awoke in a haze of well-being that belied all her fears from last night. Her asleep brain had told her that everything was all right, and that she was a superwoman. Fire-breathing dragons, sheer cliff faces, bosses and gunfights at the OK Corral. No problem.

Funnily enough, her awake brain didn't disagree, even if it was sceptical about the existence of fire-breathing dragons. They had a doctor here now. And replacement drugs. Someone who would give clear leadership and hopefully set the clinic back on the right path.

And if that someone was Jaye, then it looked as if they were both going to have to handle that as if he'd never kissed her, and she hadn't liked it so much.

'Right. That's not the problem.' She muttered the words, trying to get the disobedient haze of well-being to face facts. Kissing him wasn't the issue. Wanting to do it again—dreaming about doing it again, no less—*that* was the problem.

'Not going to happen.' Megan rolled over in bed, burying her face in the pillow. She'd work up a little healthy disbelief in the idea that today was going to be a walk in the park before she got up. That way, she couldn't be disappointed.

A tap sounded on the sliding doors of her bedroom. The small bungalows each had a sitting room at the front and a bedroom at the back, which gave out onto a veranda. Megan had never set foot on hers, since all her time in the past month had been spent working, and if anyone wanted her they knocked at the front.

'Megan…?' Jaye's voice.

Get that smile off your face, Megan. It was bad enough that she didn't mind that he'd decided to come round to the back and knock, instead of banging on the front door the way everyone else did. Liking it was beyond unacceptable.

'What?' At least she could sound unwelcoming, even if she didn't feel that way.

'You're awake?' From his cheerful tone, he clearly wasn't put off by her lukewarm welcome.

'No, I talk in my sleep. What do you want?'

'Have you got the stocktaking chart we were using last night? I can't find it anywhere.'

So he was up already and had gone across to the stockroom to start work. Megan looked at her watch, and realised that it was well past the time she'd said she would meet him there.

'Sorry. I overslept. I have it here.' Untangling herself from the sheet and drawing back the mosquito net, she grabbed the chart from the top drawer of the chest beside her bed. Megan wrapped herself up in her dressing gown and opened the sliding doors a crack, trying not to disturb the curtains as she did so.

When she posted the chart through the crack, she felt someone on the other side of the door take hold of it. Jaye was just inches away, and the *everything's all right* feeling suddenly kicked in again, this time with a vengeance.

'Don't lose it. This is my only copy.' Megan struggled with a smile, failing to keep it out of her voice.

'I'll guard it with my life.'

'Don't do that. Just don't lose it.'

She heard Jaye's quiet chuckle from behind the drapes and let go of the chart. It was about time she did something to dispel this early morning haze and got ready for the realities of the day.

CHAPTER EIGHT

THE REALITIES OF the day were almost as good as the pink, scented haze that Megan had woken up in. Someone to help with the lonely task of sorting through boxes and noting down the expiry dates on each batch of drugs. Jaye's height and strength, the way he mucked in and lifted the heavier boxes, made the work a lot less physically demanding, and his quiet humour made it a lot more pleasant. When he left to make his rounds of the clinic in-patients, the feeling that she finally had some support persisted.

'Dr Jayananda would like to see you on the ward.' Jaye had sent one of the ward helpers to relay the message.

'What does he need me for?'

The young girl shrugged. She hadn't asked and Megan probably shouldn't either. Jaye knew what she was doing and his decision was that her presence on the ward was more important. That was what a man in charge did.

He was in the small room where the young boy with dengue fever was being treated. Jaye was on one side of the bed, talking quietly to the boy's mother in Sinhalese. Megan caught the gist of the conversation, a report on how the boy was doing, but from the mother's face and Jaye's body language there was clearly a good deal of reassurance going on that her Sinhalese wasn't up to yet.

'How is he?' Megan had waited for Jaye to finish talking with the boy's mother before she advanced into the room.

'Better. He still has a fever, but the bleeding's stopped now. He's getting stronger.' The boy moved restively in the bed, and Jaye soothed him, his fingers caressing his brow. Whatever bad dreams he was having seemed to fade at Jaye's touch.

'You wanted me?' The circle of warmth that Jaye created so effortlessly wasn't what she was there for.

'You haven't had an opportunity to see him yet. After all your efforts yesterday…' He smiled. 'Or are you one of those nurses who doesn't much like finding out how her patients are doing?'

'Are there any nurses like that?' Jaye was just being a good boss. He wanted her there to give her the reward of seeing that little Ashan was better now.

'I haven't met any yet. Maybe you're one of a kind?' He moved away from the bed, letting Megan take his place at Ashan's bedside.

'No, I'm just your standard everyday nurse.' Megan leaned over the boy, touching his forehead. She didn't need temperature charts or monitors to tell that he was better, he was much quieter and the delirium that had tainted his sleep yesterday had abated.

'I was hoping you might be.' Jaye's voice came from behind her. When Megan turned he seemed to be watching her every move, and she shivered. She turned back to little Ashan and smiled at his mother to show that she too was pleased with his progress.

Five precious minutes, watching the boy sleep. Jaye had mercifully left her to it, but when she tore herself away from the child, he was waiting outside the room.

'Walk with me.'

He led her out of the clinic building and into the compound, stopping under a massive mahogany tree and leaning against its trunk.

'I've decided where my office is going to be.'

Megan looked around. She didn't see an office anywhere. 'I thought you'd take Dr Clarke's office.'

'No, that's going to be for Dr Stone when he arrives. My office will be here.'

'Under a tree?' Actually, the idea wasn't a bad one. He was visible here, and approachable. It was exactly what the clinic needed, transparent and open leadership.

'Yes. The open air's nice, don't you think?'

'You'll be getting a bit wet. The rainy season will be here any day.'

'Dinesh is going to put some duckboards down and string up an awning. In fact, rain's part of the plan. I get people in here and they can't leave without getting soaked.'

'They can't slam the door either.' Megan smiled up at him. Even her bad behaviour didn't seem so bad that she couldn't joke about it now.

Jaye chuckled quietly. 'So you like it?'

'I think it'll do very nicely. I'll come and see you here when you have a moment.'

'If you don't, I'll find you.'

Megan felt herself redden a little. There were some aspects of yesterday that she couldn't bring herself to joke about. 'I won't make that mistake again.'

'No. Neither will I.'

'Okay. Just to make things easy, you'll probably find me in the stock cupboard for the next couple of days.' Megan quite liked the idea that Jaye might come to her.

'Noted. First place I'll look.'

It was as if a well-mannered hurricane had hit the clinic, eating up the atmosphere of discord and leaving calm in its wake. Jaye started out by talking with everyone and listening to what they had to say. Even that made a difference, as the absentee level dropped suddenly and there was no more wondering who was going to turn up to work and who wasn't. And when he was done with talking, he started to make things happen.

Now that the many other worries had been lifted from her shoulders, Megan worked with a will, finishing the stock-take and disposing of anything that was out of date. After two more days closeted in the drugs cupboard, she emerged to find the clinic a very different place from the one where she'd arrived a month ago.

The atmosphere felt quieter, more peaceful somehow. Everyone knew exactly what they were supposed to do, and the daily grumbles that Megan had heard amongst the staff were beginning to subside. Ranjini's smile was far more in evidence.

She walked across the compound towards the tree. There had been some improvements. Dinesh had strung up a tarpaulin and a mosquito net for the evenings. There were two wicker chairs and a low table, and Jaye was sitting in one of the chairs.

Since he didn't have a door, she knocked on the trunk of the tree. Jaye looked up from the papers that he was reading and smiled.

'I came… I heard that you're making some changes. I'd like you to fill me in on the ones that might affect me.'

'Of course.' Jaye rose, waving her to the empty chair. He seemed pleased to see her, and Megan wondered whether he'd been waiting for her to come. Waiting for her to keep her promise, so that he could keep his.

'Would you like some iced tea?' He reached under the table, inspecting the contents of an ice bucket.

'No, thanks. Don't let me stop you, though.'

He shook his head, leaning back in his chair. 'I'm glad you came, Megan. There are a few things I'd like to discuss with you. And some news that I'd like to share, because I feel that all the staff who worked with Dr Clarke have a right to know.'

'Is something the matter?' Megan shivered, feeling guilty about all the times she'd cursed Dr Clarke's behaviour in her head.

'Yes, but now we know about it, we're hoping we'll be able to help him. The problems here came as a surprise to us because Dr Clarke had worked with us for some years in Indonesia and had an excellent track record. But it seems that his marriage was in difficulties and he had been self-medicating with increasing doses of sleeping pills and amphetamines.'

Suddenly, things began to make sense. Dr Clarke's uncertain temper and mood swings, the way he used to lock himself in his bungalow for hours, even when he was needed at the clinic. How he'd neglected most of the administrative side of his job, leaving a large pile of paperwork for Megan to pick up as soon as she'd arrived.

'And then his wife became ill?'

'That was the reason he gave for going back to London. It wasn't true. Things just got too much for him and he needed to go home.'

Megan shook her head. 'I wish we'd known. We could have at least tried to help him.'

'I don't think…' Jaye's gaze grew suddenly softer. 'From what I hear, you *did* try to help him. You picked up a lot of the things that he'd neglected and smoothed over a lot of the discord that he created.'

'I didn't know what else to do. Looking back, I just facilitated his behaviour when I should perhaps have called him on it.'

'That was our responsibility, not yours. And there was no way you could have known. It seems that Dr Clarke had been taking the drugs for a while—it all started when he was at home for a year before he came here. He was good at covering up.'

'It's… I hope he finds his way through this.'

'We're doing all we can to support him and his wife. John Ferris only found out the full extent of the problem yesterday, and he phoned me and told me last night.'

This…this was why it was so important that she stay strong. That Jaye stay strong. Because if they failed, if they allowed their personal lives to take over, there were consequences that didn't bear thinking about.

'Thank you for telling me.' Her own voice was little more than a whisper. 'It's…a lesson, I suppose. For all of us.'

'Yes, it is.'

Silence curled around them. Maybe Jaye was making the same resolutions that she was. The damage would be repaired.

'So…what next? How do we move forward from this?'

He smiled. 'I was hoping you'd ask. I've offered Ranjini a new post as director of the clinic, and she's accepted.'

'That's great news. I'm so pleased for her.'

Jaye nodded. 'Yes, and long overdue. She's going to be training a new senior nursing officer and transitioning into her own role over the next two months, and I'll be staying here to work with her over that time.'

There was a hint of awkwardness in his tone. Megan wasn't sure how she would have reacted to the news before now, but she'd seen how much good he'd done already.

'That's good. We need you here, Jaye.'

'Thank you. And as for you…' He grinned. 'I'd like you to be more involved in the clinical side and to see more of the practical problems that people here face. Ranjini's going to be looking at ways she feels we can expand our services and I want you to liaise very closely with her on that. She's taking on a lot, and she'll need all the help you can give her.'

'Thank you. When can I get started?' Megan grinned back. This was all that she'd hoped this job would be. And Jaye had made it happen.

'Speak to Ranjini tomorrow. In the meantime, I'm going to be doing some home visits every Friday. I'd like you to come along with me at the end of this week.'

'Not Dr Stone? He'll be here by then.'

'No, I'm easing him in gently. His clinical skills are excellent and he's enthusiastic, but he doesn't have much experience of working outside the UK. I'm keeping him here for a few weeks while he finds his feet. Ranjini's going to be supervising him. I want that relationship to be clear from the start.'

Jaye had thought of everything. And it was all falling into place. He was a great boss. Or at least he would be as soon as she could stop thinking about how great he might be in bed. And that was just a matter of time and concentrating her mind on other things.

'Thank you. I'd like to come with you.'

'Good. Any issues you'd like to disagree with me about?'

Megan grinned. 'No. I'm picking my battles. I'll let you know when something really big comes to mind.'

CHAPTER NINE

FRIDAY MORNING DAWNED bright and clear, after the first really big storm of the rainy season during the night. The clinic's medical outreach truck had been loaded the night before, and there was only enough time to grab a coffee and a piece of toast before she saw Jaye walk across the compound with Ranjini. They were talking together, her sari bright against his loose white shirt and pale chinos.

He leaned against the door of the truck, still talking, the keys dangling loosely from his hand. In the last few days Megan had learned that he and Ranjini discussed everything, and the easy, friendly way they did it was setting the tone for everyone else. And if jealousy nudged at her heart every time she saw Jaye talking things through with someone else, she could remind herself how hard she'd fought to be just another member of the team in his eyes.

'Ready to go?' He and Ranjini had shared a joke, and remnants of its warmth still lingered in his face.

'Yes, I'm good.' Megan opened the passenger door before Jaye could move. Today, working alone with him, she had to be on her best behaviour. And just another member of the team.

It was a special kind of torture. The clinic compound gave Jaye a certain amount of freedom because he knew that he was never truly alone with Megan. But out here, on the empty road, there probably wasn't another living soul for miles. Today would test all their good resolutions to the limit.

Perhaps he shouldn't have suggested they do this so soon. But that would be falling short of the task he'd set himself. He was determined to set the clinic to rights, have it running the way that it should, and that included giving Megan the opportunities that had been promised and which, so far, she hadn't had.

As they wound their way up into the mountains, the track grew muddier, evidence of heavier rain in the last few days. Megan's head was turned away from him, her gaze glued on the surrounding countryside.

'You haven't been up here before?'

'No, I haven't. It's beautiful.'

'Yes.' Jaye didn't want to think about beautiful right now. Not while he was sitting so close to Megan in the cabin of the truck. 'It can be unforgiving at times.'

'I imagine so.' She didn't turn to look at him. 'Where are we headed first?'

'We'll follow up on Ashan.' The boy with dengue fever had been released from the clinic the previous day, and Jaye had promised to call in on him and see how he was doing. 'There are a couple of long-term patients in the same village who I also want to look in on. Landmine victims.'

'You provide social care, as well as medical care?' She turned to him suddenly, smiling. 'I saw in the clinic's accounts that there were expenses marked "training and development".'

'Yes, we do. Although I'm not entirely sure where the line between the two lies.'

'No, me neither.' Megan turned her head back towards the window, and Jaye concentrated on the road.

The rest of their journey was made in silence, but when they reached the village Megan seemed suddenly more animated. She followed him from the truck, drinking in everything around her. The clay-brick houses, with thatched roofs extending over porches that were often larger than the houses themselves, providing a living area for each family. The well-tended gardens, and lush vegetation that provided food. The men who approached Jaye to greet him, the women and children standing further back but watching all the same.

When they came to Ashan's home, Jaye hung back, waiting to see what Megan would do. The boy's mother welcomed her, and she exchanged a few smiling pleasantries in Sinhalese. The boy was resting in the shade of the porch, and although Megan clearly didn't understand his chatter, the warmth was obvious. As she nodded and smiled at the boy, her fingers brushed his cheek, checking for any fever.

'How is he?' Jaye had been watching, trying not to be entranced by her.

'I think he said he's happy to be home. He seems happy to be home.' Megan looked up at him. 'Are you taking a look at him?'

'I thought you might do that.'

'Will you ask his mother how he's been?'

Jaye didn't move. He wanted to see how Megan coped on her own.

Her lips narrowed into a line. Any reaction from Megan, even if it was a frown, felt better than her studied professionalism. He was going to have to be careful.

'My Sinhalese isn't good enough. I might miss something she says.' She picked up the medical bag from where it lay at his feet and flapped her hand at him, chivvying him along. 'Come on. Pull your weight, Jaye.'

'This is how you treat your boss?' He couldn't help grinning.

'You asked for it.'

Yes, he had. After the last time he'd pushed her and gone too far, doing it again seemed like a hazardous process, but it seemed to be working out. *She* was making it work.

He watched out of the corner of his eye, talking to Ashan's mother, while Megan carefully checked the boy over, taking his blood pressure and listening to his chest. When she'd finished, and packed up the bag, he waited for her verdict.

'What does his mother say?' Clearly she wasn't going to give it until she had all the information.

'No problems. They're giving him the medication we sent him home with.'

'In that case, I'd say he's doing well. Shall I put him on the list for a follow-up next Friday?'

It probably wasn't necessary. The people here had all seen dengue fever before and knew when to come to the doctor. But he'd asked her to examine Ashan and she'd decided to err on the side of safety. He shouldn't second-guess her.

'Yes. We'll do that.'

Another test. Megan was used to being tested in new situations, most people waited until they could get the measure of the new member of staff. Jaye was no different, and if it made Megan nervous, that was her lookout. She pulled the strap of the heavy medical bag across her shoulder, daring him to take it back from her.

Every action, every word had to be thought about. It would get easier. Just as she'd learned to be with him in the compound, she would learn to be with him out here. It was just a matter of practice.

He gave her the history of their second patient on the way to the next house. Then he introduced her to the young woman whose right leg had been amputated by the blast of a landmine, folded his arms and stood back.

This time Jaye seemed determined not to help when Megan's Sinhalese failed her. The woman had picked up a few words of English, clearly as a result of contact with doctors, since they all seemed to relate to her leg. Gestures and smiles filled the gaps and they got by. Megan satisfied herself that the woman was managing her prosthetic leg well, and that it was causing no blisters or sores, and then moved on to the baby she was nursing, for good measure.

All the time she felt that Jaye's gaze was boring into her back, assessing and evaluating everything she did. When she turned to leave he asked a question in Sinhalese, which was too rapid for Megan to catch the meaning of. The woman smiled and replied and Jaye laughed. Her husband joined in the conversation, which for some reason seemed to centre around cushions. Then a smiling goodbye.

She laboured up the dirt track with Jaye, struggling a little with the weight of the bag but determined not to give it up to him. In return, he was giving her no quarter and she had to break into a stumbling jog to keep up.

'Wait… Wait!' She stopped short, heaving the strap of the medical bag onto the other shoulder.

'Can I take that?'

It wasn't an unreasonable offer, and it was entirely expected from Jaye. Megan was surprised he hadn't tackled her to the ground and wrestled the bag away from her, just to satisfy his own good manners. But now she had it, she wasn't going to give it up.

'No. But you can stop a moment and tell me what you were saying to her.'

He shrugged. 'It was nothing. We were just discussing the work that she does.'

'Cushions? She makes cushions?' Megan wanted to let him know that she'd followed at least part of the conversation.

'Yes. One of my mother's projects. She imports hand-crafted goods from areas like these and sells them. She's got a website. And it's cushion *covers*, there's no point in filling up a container full of stuffed cushions when you can perfectly easily pack the covers into a small trunk.'

'It would have been useful if you'd mentioned it. It's always good to know what patients do for a living.'

'In case she suffers from some kind of industrial sewing injury, you mean?' His lip curled slightly. 'My mother doesn't work like that.'

'I'm sure she doesn't. But if she's doing a lot of close work, I might think it was a good idea to have a brief look at her eyes, even if the clinic's optician visits every six months.'

'You know about that?'

'I went through the books to do a couple of reports for Dr Clarke that London was asking for.'

'Ah. Well, yes, the optician will be visiting. I'll make a note to check on exactly when.'

They were getting nowhere fast. They had got used to working alongside each other, but that wasn't enough out here.

'Jaye, just hold on a minute.' He'd turned, ready to start walking again, and Megan stopped him. 'I know what you're doing, and I appreciate that you're allowing me to create my own relationships with the people here. But I need you to help me. My Sinhalese isn't good enough yet, and I'm afraid I'll miss something.'

'I can translate anything you ask me to.'

'I need to…rely on you.' These were dangerous waters. The last time she'd relied on him, wanting to hear his every word, see his every reaction, it had led them into an intimacy that Megan couldn't handle.

The look in his eyes told her that he didn't want to go there either. Maybe he was thinking the same as she was, that the last time they'd acknowledged the special connection that buzzed between them they'd been in each other's arms. But if they could just move on from that and find it in themselves to harness that connection, who knew what energy they could create? Who knew what they could do?

There was a long silence and then Jaye spoke. 'Yes. You're right. We'll make a good team. Give me the bag.'

'What?'

'The bag. Working together, remember?'

'Oh. Yes.' She handed the heavy medical bag over, careful not to brush against him as she did so. It was actually quite a relief not to have to carry it any further.

'Good.' He smiled at her, and started walking again. Megan stumbled after him.

'So… Our next patient? What's the story?'

'He's a seven-year-old boy. He lost a hand and the lower part of his arm in another landmine explosion.'

'Seven years old? I thought that all the landmines had been cleared in this area. Was this one that was left behind?'

'Yes and no. They've all been cleared and this wasn't one that was left behind. Chaminda was just a baby, in his mother's arms. His mother stepped on the mine and her body shielded Chaminda from most of the blast. She was killed.'

'So that means that the family's not just coping with their son's injury, they're doing it without their mother.'

'Yes. The father usually comes up with a load of questions about his other children as well. He's naturally very protective, and he worries that he isn't doing a good job of raising them.' He grinned. 'Although this *is* a village.'

'And it takes a village to raise a child?'

'Well, in this case, the village is doing a pretty good job of it. But the father still worries.'

'I guess he'll probably have a lot to say to me, then.'

Jaye nodded. 'Almost certainly. I'll translate as we go.'

'What about Chaminda? Have we been doing anything about providing him with a prosthetic hand?'

'That's an issue too. We've offered one, but since he's grown up with only one hand, he manages very well without a prosthetic. It's a delicate balance. The family needs to make their own decisions about that, but we want to keep his options open for the future.'

'What's Chaminda been offered? And what are the pros and cons, as you see them?'

Megan had suggested an audacious solution to a problem that had become increasingly apparent during the course of the morning. A meeting of minds that had been born in the heat of an embrace. Working together, and not just side by side.

But it had worked. She'd examined Chaminda and talked at length with her young patient's father, Jaye translating for her. They'd both made suggestions, and Jaye felt that they'd made some good progress in helping the family.

It was exhausting, though. Jaye was almost pleased to be able to get back into the truck so that they could both find some refuge in silence.

But the silence didn't last long. As they rounded a corner, climbing the steep slope that led to the next village, he jammed on the brakes, managing to stop just inches away from the pile of mud and stones across the road.

They both took a moment to catch their breath then Megan glanced towards him.

'Landslip?'

'Yes. It's probably been dislodged by last night's rain. But don't worry, this area's been combed for landmines and the road's been safe for years.'

'Then we can just get on and clear it?'

Jaye nodded. They were going to have to make a path through the debris as they couldn't go around the stones because of the steep slope rising up to the left and falling down to the right of the road.

'Yes. Shouldn't be too difficult. I think we can just roll that out of the way...' He pointed to the right-hand side of the road where a heavy mass of earth, bound together by tree roots, blocked their path.

Jaye got out of the truck and walked across to the boulder. When he set his weight against it and then heaved, the boulder moved three inches and then fell back two.

'I need you to help me...' If Megan added her weight to his, the boulder would move. The process might involve touching her, but that couldn't be helped.

'Right. Where do you want me?'

There was a good answer to that question. A very good one. Jaye took the second-best option and pointed to the right-hand side of the boulder.

'Just there. Put your shoulder to it when I say.'

He found a handhold on the side of the boulder and they both pushed. Nothing happened. Jaye leant further in, feeling the warmth of her body, and the boulder slid a couple of feet.

'Okay, stop a moment.' He checked again that if the boulder tipped over and rolled down the slope to their right, there would be nothing in its path. The slope levelled out after twenty feet and a pile of rubble was already lodged at the bottom of it.

'One more try...'

They pushed hard, a cry of effort escaping Megan's lips. The boulder slid to the edge of the slope and suddenly the handhold that Jaye had found gave way. A sharp pain shot up his arm as his hand caught in a matted tree root, almost dragging his little finger off. His grunt of pain caught Megan's attention and she whirled around.

'What...?' She was off balance, and as the boulder started to roll down the slope, the momentum of her own body carried her after it. At the last moment she threw herself to the ground, trying to stop herself from toppling down the slope.

'Megan...!' The pain in his hand was forgotten. Everything was forgotten because although Megan had managed to stop herself from falling, she was sliding over the edge, scrabbling for a hold in the mud. Jaye ran to where she'd been standing, dropping to his knees.

CHAPTER TEN

A SMALL INCOHERENT cry came from below him. She'd managed to twist round and find a handhold and she was lying on her stomach, her feet sending chunks of mud and stones down the slope as she tried to find a firm foothold.

'Still. Be still.'

She obeyed him immediately, her gaze fixed on his face, the message in her eyes clear. *Don't let me fall.*

The fall wouldn't kill her, but it could well hurt her. The boulder had broken up on the way down and sharp stones and tangled tree roots littered the slope.

Jaye lay flat on the ground, reaching for her, his fingers just a few inches from her frightened eyes. He felt a searing pain as he grabbed hold of a tree root with his other hand but swallowed it, inching forward and reaching down with the other arm.

'Okay. I've got you Megan.' He curled his fingers around the top of her arm. He wasn't going to let go, and if she fell now, he would be going with her.

For one moment her gaze locked with his. They weren't going to fall.

'Let go. Hold onto me.' She had to trust him now. Suddenly that didn't seem as if it would be so difficult for her.

He felt her hand, gripping his arm, just above the elbow.

'Good. That's good, Megan. Now try to find a foothold. Gently… There's one about six inches to your right.'

She didn't answer but Jaye knew she'd do it. She was staring at him, her foot moving slowly in the direction he'd indicated.

'Got it.'

'Okay. Can you push yourself up a little?' Lying flat on his stomach, Jaye didn't have the leverage to pull her up. All he could do was provide a firm hold for her to climb by herself.

'Yes, I can do it.' He felt her move, and she grabbed his shoulder with her other hand. It was as if they were moving slowly into an embrace.

'Good. A little bit more, Megan.'

She moved again, closer still. He could feel her cheek against his. Waiting until she had got both hands on his shoulders, he wound his arm around her back.

'I've got you.' Carefully he rolled over, pulling her up the slope and away from the edge. He felt the sweet weight of her body on his and held her tight on top of him. Professionalism be damned, he wasn't going to let her go now. She could put that down to the clinic director being unwilling to lose his best nurse if she wanted to.

'Oh. Thank you… Thank you.' She was still clinging to him, seemingly unaware of how his body was reacting, hardening against hers. Jaye held her tight, trying to stop his head from swimming.

'Okay. You're okay, Megan.'

'I'm so stupid…' Her face was grimed with mud and dust, making her eyes look even bluer. So blue that he could have plunged into them, like cool, clear water.

His hand was *really* hurting now. Perhaps that was just as well because it brought him to his senses.

'What's the matter?' She raised her head from his chest, her gaze searching his, as he twisted to inspect the damage.

'Nothing…' He frowned as he caught sight of his hand. It was something.

She levered herself up suddenly against him, and Jaye winced as a delicious reaction to the movement shot through him. For a moment he forgot all about his hand.

But Megan hadn't. She was sitting on the ground next to him, holding his wrist so that she could see his finger properly. Jaye stared at the sky, trying to ignore the feel of her fingers and not particularly wanting to look at his hand either.

'I think… It's swelling already. I think you've broken your little finger.'

Oh, well. Megan would deal with it. The thought of experiencing first-hand what it was like to be one of her patients seemed almost worth it. He wondered vaguely if he'd get the special smile. He was looking forward to that.

His eye wandered to the wide scar on the hillside above them where the earth had slipped, leaving a wide trail of mud in its wake. Suddenly, there was no question about him just lying back and letting Megan do whatever she wanted.

'Megan, look. Up there, you see where the landslip's come from, right at the top of this hill?'

'Yes?'

'Halfway down, right in its path. That's where we're going. The next village.'

She let go of his wrist and her hand flew to her mouth. Jaye scrambled to his feet.

'We need to get there. They might need help.'

'Wait. Wait, you need help as well.' She followed him to the car, grabbing his arm.

'I'm okay. There could be people seriously injured up there.'

She thought for a moment, obviously weighing up the pros and cons in her head.

'I'll see to your hand first then we'll go and take a look.' Jaye opened his mouth to protest and she fixed him with a fierce glare. 'Be quiet. This is *my* judgement call.'

She was right. She was in a much better position to assess his injury—every time he looked at his finger, hanging at an odd angle to his hand, his head swam. And he wasn't any use like this.

'All right. Strap it up so I've got use of my thumb and forefinger at least. Quickly, and then we'll go.'

'It'll take whatever time it takes…' Megan obviously knew they needed to be quick as she'd already opened the tailgate of the truck and was rummaging in the back for the things she needed. By the time he'd walked unsteadily around to join her, she was splashing water over her hands and opening the zip of her sweatshirt to dry them on her T-shirt, which was at least mostly clean. Then she donned a pair of surgical gloves.

'Sit.' She pointed to the open back of the vehicle, and Jaye obeyed her. 'You're going to have to just grit your teeth for this bit.'

He knew that. Any analgesic that would work fast enough to make a difference to the pain now would leave him feeling too groggy to be of any use later.

'Just get on with it.'

'All right. Wait…' She'd slowed now, carefully feeling along each of his fingers, assessing the damage.

'Okay, it's definitely broken. I'm going to splint it temporarily until we get back to the clinic and we can X-ray it.' She gave him the smile. The one that seemed to make all her patients feel a little better. It hit him hard, making him forget the pain as she deftly applied the finger splint.

* * *

He'd done exactly as she'd told him. Maybe he was in shock. Or maybe he'd felt it too, that sudden connection that had shot between them when it had seemed almost inevitable that she would slide away from him, down the slope. She'd asked him to work with her, but their conscious minds had only been able to go so far in breaking down the barriers. It had taken this one moment of panic to shatter them, and it had rocked them both to the core.

Careful what you wish for. She checked that the dressing she'd applied over the splint to immobilise the side of his hand wasn't too tight. That was going to have to do. If they got to the village and found that all was well, she could re-dress it then.

'How does it feel?'

She'd treated broken bones plenty of times before, and in Africa she'd done so with fewer medical supplies than she had available now. But not Jaye's bones. Not with the adrenaline of having him haul her out of danger and into his arms running in her veins. Not with the scent of his body teasing her like a mischievous sprite.

'Much better, thanks.' He held up his hand, waggling his thumb and forefinger in answer to her next question.

'Good. Let's go, then. Where are the keys?' She collected up the roll of tape and the scissors and bundled them back into the medical bag.

He pulled the keys out of his pocket, frowning slightly, as if he was thinking about what to do with them. Then he handed them over.

'I'll guide you across.' Jaye stood up, stretching his limbs slightly.

'Sure you're okay? You don't feel dizzy or anything?'

They were in a hurry, but having him keel over on her wasn't going to make things any quicker.

'I'm fine. There's a track that leads up to those houses a couple of miles further along the road. Let's go.'

He guided her through the mud and rocks on the road, and Megan inched forward, careful not to go anywhere near the slope on her right. The track that branched off the road, leading to the houses, was bumpy and potholed but Jaye's sharp eyes and quiet directions meant that they made it without getting stuck. As Megan drove up to the small group of houses, arranged around a dirt compound, her heart sank.

Three of the houses were untouched. A fourth had taken some damage to the roof, and a fifth was almost completely buried, one side of the roof sticking out from a mass of mud and rubble. And there were people digging, men, women and children using their hands and whatever tools were available to make a path through the debris.

'There must be someone in there.' Jaye had opened the passenger door almost before she drew to a halt, and he swung out of the truck, jogging towards one of the men who seemed to be directing operations. A brief conversation, and he was back again.

'There's a woman and three of her children inside. They've heard the baby crying and the woman calling for help.'

'Is everyone all right?'

'One of the children is hurt. They don't know how badly.' Jaye strode to the back of the truck, opening the tailgate, and one of the men pulled out a large canvas bag and unzipped it. Inside Megan could see a couple of shovels and a tarpaulin, obviously intended to dig the truck out of the mud if need be.

'Can you help dig?' He held out one of the shovels and Megan nodded, taking it. 'We're going to try to get a rope around that big piece there and tow it out of the way.'

At least he wasn't going to try and dig one-handed. She left him uncoiling a piece of rope from the bag, and joined the line of people who were toiling to move the pile of debris at one side of the house.

As she started to dig, it began to rain heavily, and within moments she was soaked to the skin. It would have been a relief from the heat if there hadn't been the worry of water and mud trickling down into the house from above.

The rain stopped as suddenly as it had started, leaving the workers struggling and slipping in the mud. When Megan straightened for a moment, her back aching, she felt a hand flutter against her arm, and a tiny old woman offered her a hot drink in a patterned china cup. She drank the warm, sweet tea down, thanking the woman in Sinhalese, and got back to work.

Megan was vaguely aware that Jaye was directing the operation to get the tarpaulin and ropes around a large, solid mass of rock and earth that blocked one side of the house. The tarpaulin had slipped once, dragged down by the rain and the mud, but the men had wasted no time with dismay, just shaken their heads and started all over again.

'Please, miss. Over there, if you please.' She'd finished helping shovel away the debris on one side of the boulder and had barely caught her breath when the man from the village who was directing the diggers pointed to another place that needed work.

'Thanks.' Megan trudged over to the spot he'd indicated, turning as she heard Jaye call from the direction of the truck.

'Don't wear yourself out. I'll be needing you later.' He was almost a head taller than most of the men around him, a natural leader who expected more from himself than he did from anyone around him. Powerful, with a raw edge of grace, which gave him the air of a warrior king. Jaye's assertion that it was only the chance accident of his birth that had made him any different was wrong. Understandable maybe, but wrong.

'I don't have time for a break. Will you take mine for me?'

He smiled, heaving on the ropes that were being fixed to the tow bar of the truck. 'Will do. When I get the chance.'

Another fifteen minutes, and they were ready. Everyone stood back, the muffled sound of a baby crying breaking the silence. Jaye carefully edged the truck forward, stopping for a long moment to allow the men to adjust the ropes.

A disappointed groan sounded through the knot of people, families gathered together all holding their breath, as a large crack formed in the boulder. For a moment it seemed it might break apart, but it held for long enough for Jaye to edge forward another couple of inches.

'Enough… It's enough.' A hole had opened up that was large enough for Megan to squeeze through. It would be tight, but she could make it.

Jaye glanced over his shoulder. 'I think it'll take a little more.'

He revved the engine, moving forward again, and the hole increased in size. Then the crack in the boulder widened and the whole of the top collapsed, the crisscross of ropes and the tarpaulin pulling the debris forward and away from the house.

Jaye climbed from the driver's seat, calling for quiet. The only sound was that of the baby.

'I'll go…'

Jaye paused and then nodded. Handing her the flashlight, his hand brushed her arm, and she felt the tiny hairs at the back of her neck stand on end.

'Just be careful.'

Jaye watched as Megan crawled across the shattered rubble that formed the lower part of the boulder. He knew that this was the right decision. There was no question that one of them had to go to give medical aid to the family trapped inside the house. He just wished that it could have been him.

But even if his hand hadn't been injured, he wouldn't have fitted through the hole. Jaye held his breath as Megan perched the flashlight at the mouth of the hole and reached in. Good. Someone inside must have been able to reach up to her and maybe she wouldn't have to go down there.

A long moment of silence, with the whole village holding its breath. Then Megan drew back, a bundle of bright fabric in her arms. Passing the baby back to the man behind her, she turned again, steadying herself to reach back into the hole.

Jaye quickly checked the baby for any signs of bleeding. It was crying lustily, its airways quite obviously clear, and he allowed one of the older women to take it and rock it gently in her arms.

Then another excited gasp came from the knot of people as Megan slid back from the hole, a little boy of about four held tightly in her arms. Jaye thought he saw Megan brush a kiss against his cheek before she passed him back down the line.

The boy was covered in mud, the only part of his skin visible being the streaks on his cheeks from tears. He obediently showed Jaye a minor cut on his leg, and Jaye examined the wound quickly, asking the boy in Sinhalese if anything had fallen on him, and was he hurt anywhere else.

The boy shook his head, a silent, grey ghost in the sunshine. He seemed physically okay, and Jaye handed him over to his father for a tearful hug, before one of the women took charge, leading him away to sit on the steps of a nearby veranda.

'The other child's hurt. The mother's not coming out without her.' There was no need for Megan to tell him what she was going to do next.

'We will bring them to you.' It was the only promise he could give to a husband who had seen two of his children emerge relatively unscathed from the rubble of his home, and who was almost frantic with fear for his wife and third child. Jaye signalled to two of the other men, who held the man back, trying to keep him calm.

Jaye scrambled past the line of men to the mouth of the hole. Megan had already lowered her feet into the hole, and he braced his feet against the mud and rocks, winding his good arm around her waist.

'Hold onto me…' A flashlight had been passed down to the woman inside the house, but its beam was moving jerkily and no help in seeing what was down there. Megan wrapped her arms around his neck and he lowered her down.

'Okay. I've got a foothold.' Megan almost whispered the words against his cheek. 'Let me go… Jaye, let me go now.'

If he lost her, he'd lose himself. The thought flashed through his mind and, despite all his instincts to keep a tight hold on her, he let her slide downwards, into the darkness.

He heard the sounds of movement and then the beam of the torch steadied. Six feet below him Jaye could see the mother, her sari soaked in blood, holding her child on her lap.

'She won't let go of her… Tell her I have to see her.' Megan seemed to know he was there even though she hadn't looked around.

He quickly translated the words into Sinhalese, adding the information that Megan was a nurse and that she could help. The woman loosened her grip on her daughter, allowing Megan to gently examine her.

'Airways are clear… She's breathing… There's a bad cut on her leg, it may be broken. She's lost a lot of blood.'

Jaye turned, signalling for the medical bag, which had been fetched and was ready behind him. He lowered it down to Megan and she unzipped it.

'The dressing pads are on the left-hand side…' Jaye knew that the next thing that Megan had to do was stem the bleeding.

'Right. Got them. As soon as I can stop the bleeding, we need to get her out of here.'

'Okay, we're ready.'

The woman was rocking and crying, still holding her daughter. Megan bound the dressings over a gash in the child's leg and she screamed in pain. The mother clung to her child.

'Okay… Tell her I'm sorry, and that I had to stop the bleeding. And I need some room down here.'

Jaye translated quickly, telling the woman that she must go now to make room to lower the stretcher down, and she shook her head.

Megan understood that. 'Tell her… No, ask her to let me take care of her daughter. I will treat her as if she were my own child.'

And Megan would. There was no doubt in Jaye's mind that she would do anything to protect the little girl. He translated the words into Sinhalese and the woman hesitated, and then nodded.

If Megan's words hadn't been enough to convince the woman, her fierce and loving determination were. Megan took the little girl from her arms and the men beside Jaye reached down, helping to pull the woman up to safety. A line of willing hands helped her across the pile of rubble to her husband.

Jaye called for the stretcher and the folding cot from the truck was lowered into the hole. 'Check her again, Megan.' Speed was essential, but it was also critical to make sure that the girl had no other injuries.

'Okay. Done. She's been moving around down here but I've put a collar on her.' Megan had snapped the cot open and was securing the child in it. 'Make it quick. The dressings haven't completely stopped the bleeding and we need to keep pressure up on the wound.'

'I'll take her, and you follow with the medical bag.' Jaye wanted to lift Megan back up to safety himself, to feel her arms around him and to know that she was all right. But his first duty lay with their patient, and he knew that Megan would understand.

'Righty. See you there.'

Jaye supervised the men at the mouth of the hole and they hauled the cot up, carrying it carefully to the shade of a veranda. He bent down beside the child, checking her pulse, and then clamped his hand over the dressings on her leg.

'Saline.' He heard footsteps behind him and knew they were Megan's. 'We have some in the back of the truck.'

'Okay.' She was back again in less than a minute, carrying the bag that contained everything they needed to set up a saline drip.

'What's her pulse like?' Megan snapped on a pair of surgical gloves, gripping the dressings over the girl's leg and using her free hand to help Jaye pull a glove onto his good hand.

'Fast. Weak. She's bleeding out.' Jaye glanced up into Megan's eyes. 'Follow my lead…'

She was his left hand, and he was her right. Together

they managed to insert the catheter and set up a line to the saline. They were a team…no, a dream team…each knowing what the other was about to do.

'We'll replace the dressings?'

Jaye nodded. Blood was oozing out of the hastily applied dressing, and although Megan had done a good job, they could do better now.

He gripped the saline bag between the thumb and forefinger of his injured hand, holding it up to get as much fluid into the girl's veins as quickly as possible. It would keep her alive for long enough, until they could get her back to the clinic to administer blood. Pain shot up his arm and he winced.

'Okay?' Megan's gaze found his and Jaye nodded.

Quickly she reapplied the dressings while Jaye pressed hard on the girl's leg to stem the flow of blood. One more check, to make sure that she was stable, and they were ready to go. Jaye transferred the saline bag to his other hand, and the pain in his fingers subsided to a fierce ache.

The stretcher bearers stepped forward from the circle of people around them, lifting the cot carefully and taking it to the truck to secure it on the back seat. Jaye felt almost dizzy. Pain and effort would do that to you, but this was the dizziness of exhilaration. The little girl was free of the rubble and still alive. There was still a way to go before she was out of danger, but he and Megan had accomplished so much already. Together.

CHAPTER ELEVEN

JAYE WAS TALKING rapidly in Sinhalese to the girl's parents, and her father climbed into the passenger seat of the truck beside her. It seemed that the mother was staying behind in the care of the other villagers.

'Do we need to bring the other children?' Megan twisted around as Jaye settled himself in the back seat, next to the little girl.

'I gave them the once-over as they came out. And I called down to the clinic while you were digging. They're sending someone up. They'll be here soon.'

The sound of a motorbike heralded Dinesh's arrival. Perched on the back, Dr Stone, the young, sandy haired doctor who had arrived at the clinic yesterday, was looking pale but otherwise unscathed. He walked unsteadily up to the truck and a brief exchange between him and Jaye established that there was another vehicle on its way, and that Dr Stone would take charge of the rest of the family.

'So much for easing him in gently.' Megan murmured the words as she drove out of the compound, following Jaye's directions on the quickest way back to the clinic.

'He's survived the worst of it.' Jaye knew as well as she did that any medical challenges involved in looking after the family paled into insignificance next to being bumped around, riding pillion, as Dinesh took the quickest and most hair-raising route from A to B.

'Yes. Suppose so.' Megan concentrated on the track ahead of her, hoping that the girl in Jaye's care on the back seat of the truck would survive too.

Ranjini was ready when they arrived back at the clinic. Gentle hands lifted the girl from the truck, transferring her inside, while Ranjini took charge of her father, guiding him into the building. Jaye followed, beckoning to Megan.

'Help me get cleaned up.' He made a beeline for the clinic's shower room, and Megan followed him. Easy. This was going to be easy because, however many of his clothes Jaye discarded, there was an urgent need to get clean and dressed again.

He caught his breath in pain as she stripped his shirt from his back. His hand must be really hurting by now. She switched on the shower and he ducked the top half of his body under it, rivulets of dust tracking their way down to expose smooth, dark skin.

No time to think about how good it felt to touch him as she quickly soaped his hands and arms. Then she towelled him dry and he pulled one of the scrub tops from the pile, easing it carefully over his head as he made for the door.

How could one snatched glance imprint itself so indelibly? She had other concerns right now, and Megan wanted to hurry back to the girl's side, but as she gathered up the towels, putting the soap back in its holder, all she could see was Jaye. Broad shoulders, slim hips, a triangle of visual pleasure leading down to the ultimate physical pleasure.

'Stop. It.' How many times was she going to have to say this before her fantasies listened? If things had been the other way round, Jaye would have managed it without leering at her, and she should be able to give him the same consideration.

Hurrying after him, she found that Jaye was already in the emergency treatment room with Ranjini and another of the senior nurses. Blood was taken and tested for type, and an IV drip was set up. Ranjini cut the temporary dressing from the girl's leg and another was applied, with as little blood loss as could be managed. Covered in dust and grime still, all that Megan could do was press her face against the glass door and watch.

He'd worked with everyone here before, and everyone knew exactly what to do. Jaye could stand back a little, giving quiet instructions, and allow Ranjini to be his hands. It felt as if Megan's other, stronger half had been ripped away, leaving her just a pale shadow on the sidelines.

She watched as the nurses wheeled the gurney out of the emergency room in response to Jaye's call for an X-ray. Suddenly, everything that needed to be done had been done, without any input from Megan.

'I don't think the leg's broken, but we'll take an X-ray to be sure. Once she's stable I'll have Dr Stone do the stitches.' He stopped next to her, speaking as if she'd been an integral part of the process.

'How's her BP?'

'Steady. Beginning to rise a little.' He smiled. 'She's beginning to feel the pain, and I've sedated her.'

That was a good thing. The child was coming back to them, and as she did so she was starting to register pain.

'Do you need a hand with the X-ray machine? I can go and clean up.'

He grinned. 'No. Ranjini can deal with that on her own.'

She wasn't needed, even for that. And she couldn't even look Jaye in the eye, she was so afraid of what she'd see there. That he didn't need her at all. After the intensity of the connection between them it was almost physically painful.

His finger moved under her chin, tipping her head up. Megan instinctively moved to swat his hand away, but she couldn't. The warmth in his eyes wouldn't allow that.

'I could really do with some coffee, though.'

Jaye sat in the small living area of Megan's bungalow. It wasn't so different from his own as the bungalows were all built to the same plan and were furnished the same. It was the little changes that Megan had made that made it so special.

There was a bright, woven throw across the back of the small sofa, obviously from Africa. A couple of large candles on the coffee table, which Megan must have brought with her from England. He liked the fact that she'd felt the soft light warranted the space they'd take in her suitcase. And the scent of her soap, which seemed to follow him around whenever he was close to her.

Something had happened. He wasn't sure what but, whatever it was, it had changed everything. This morning they'd set out, both flinching every time the other got too close. And now...

It was if they'd been taken, shaken and then thrust together in an intimacy that should have sent Jaye running scared. At the time it had been necessary, but now he had the leisure to replay it in his head.

Her yelp sounded from the small shower room. Clearly the water was cold. The bungalows were powered by solar panels, and there was a choice between shade in the afternoons and consistently hot water. It was a design flaw, and Jaye turned his mind to how he might rectify it, in the hope that it would take his mind away from the idea that Megan must currently be naked.

It didn't. Not being able to see her now didn't mean that he didn't remember the softness of her skin against his cheek. He'd felt it again today, and somehow it had been just the same. Working with her wasn't the same as an embrace, but the two seemed to have a lot in common.

He puzzled over the thought for a while, and then Megan breezed back out of her bedroom, wearing a striped T-shirt and a clean pair of chinos. She walked over to the small kitchenette in the corner of the room and reached up into the cupboard.

'I have ground coffee…'

'Where did you get that from? Not the kitchen, surely.'

'I brought some coffee with me. I've been eking it out and this is the last of it.'

So she was sharing the last of her best coffee with him, rather than the milky instant stuff that the clinic kitchens served up. 'I'm going down to Colombo next week. I'll get you some more.'

'You're planning on driving? With that hand?'

Jaye hadn't really thought about it. 'I should think it'll be okay by then.'

Megan raised her eyebrows, pursing her lips in that delicious *I don't think so* expression. 'You'd be better taking Dinesh to do the driving.'

There it was again. Someone to notice. Someone who would care about him and boss him around a little when he needed it.

'Maybe. I'll see.'

She plonked a mug of coffee down in front of him and Jaye took a sip, savouring the rich aroma. 'So how does it feel? Your hand?'

He shrugged. 'It's okay.'

'Don't worry about me, Megan.' Her tone deepened by a couple of octaves, mimicking his. 'As Director of the Western Province Free Clinic, and Peer of the Realm, my nerve endings should be different from everyone else's. I allow myself to feel no pain.'

Jaye caught his breath, almost choking on his coffee. 'I never said that.'

'No, you never *said* it.' She sat down in the chair opposite him, her gaze challenging him to pretend that he'd never thought it.

'Okay. I'll take Dinesh with me. Happy now?'

'I'll be a lot happier when it's been X-rayed and properly splinted.'

Jaye had been figuring on doing that himself. Suddenly he wasn't. 'You'll be sorry you said that when I start crying like a baby.'

She smirked, clearly understanding that this was some kind of victory. 'I'm a nurse, crying doesn't bother me. And these will have kicked in by that time. One or two?'

She held up a blister pack of paracetamol. Jaye was suddenly tired of managing, tired of making do by himself. If he couldn't rely on Megan as a lover, he might just be able to as a newfound friend.

'I'll take the full thousand milligrams.'

'Good. My thoughts exactly.' She broke two tablets out of the pack, and handed them over to him. When he swallowed the paracetamol, washing it down with a swig of coffee and then leaning back in his seat, it felt as if he was relaxing for the first time in weeks.

Megan had let him rest for all of five minutes before ushering him back to the clinic. She then allowed him to at least supervise the X-ray procedure, reminding her of the safety protocols before they switched the machine on. Then she positioned his hand carefully on the couch. He resisted the impulse to move his fingers slightly. It would have been arrogant to do so, since she had the angle just right.

'Not bad. Not bad at all.' He grinned at her as they reviewed the X-rays together on the computer screen. He could see the break, but the finger had been straightened almost perfectly, which was no mean feat considering the conditions she'd been working under.

'Hmm. Maybe a little more.' She peered at the screen, assessing the two X-rays carefully.

'So you're going to hurt me again, are you?' Jaye would have done the same himself to ensure that the finger healed perfectly straight.

'You know it's for your own good.' That pursed-lips expression again. He was beginning to like it, because Megan's eyes were full of a humorous, almost self-mocking light. Being one of her patients seemed like the best thing in the world at the moment.

'Do I get a sweet?' He nodded towards the jar of sweets on the countertop intended to dry children's tears.

'Yeah, you get a sweet. When I'm done with you, though, and not before.'

Could it hold? Could this really hold?

Megan felt as if she were tiptoeing into new territory, into a fragile friendship built on the foundations of something completely different. Something that they'd both rejected because it was far too hard for either of them to contemplate. But the friendship was surprisingly easy, and after a few days of thinking that its foundations were made of sand and it was all going to topple in on her at any moment, Megan began to cautiously rely on it.

And Jaye made a very good friend. He never gave her any quarter professionally, never made things awkward by favouring her over any of the other staff. But he gave her the opportunities that had been promised, and ensured she made the best of them. At his behest, she and Ranjini started a review of the outreach programmes, with a view to expanding the women's services that were so dear to Ranjini's heart.

He'd remembered the coffee, returning from Colombo with half a dozen bags for her. And he must have bought some himself because the following day, when she knocked on the door of his bungalow to inspect the swelling on his hand, wash it and change the plastic sleeve that protected the splint, he had a cup ready for her.

It wasn't entirely necessary. But it was the one time in the day that Jaye kept entirely for her. Megan justified it with the knowledge that Jaye made time to speak with everyone in the clinic every day. This was just her five minutes.

'You've been washing your hands again.' She inspected the skin between his fingers, where soapy water had seeped under the plastic sleeve and inflamed the skin slightly.

'Yeah. Force of habit. I can't help it.'

'I thought you were going to let Dr Stone do the hands-on stuff and stand back for a while,' she reproved him gently.

'I'm trying.' He gave her a delicious smile, and Megan couldn't help but chuckle.

'Okay. As long as you're trying.'

'What are you up to on Friday?' He watched, uncomplaining, as Megan taped the plastic cover in place.

'I haven't got anything planned. Ranjini's interviewing for a new nurse, and I thought I'd catch up on some paperwork.'

'You've done enough paperwork already. Dinesh isn't available to drive me, so I thought you might like to come along for the home visits. We'll try to keep the digging to a minimum this time.'

It was so easy to say yes. They were entirely alone now, and Jaye treated her just the same as when they were surrounded by people.

'Thanks. I'd like to do that.'

CHAPTER TWELVE

THEY WERE MAKING it work. Not without a few awkward silences from time to time, a few things that Jaye wanted to say but which remained unsaid. Not without missing her, when she set out for a four-day tour of potential sites for the new women's clinic that she and Ranjini were setting up, and not without feeling a sharp twang of regret that he had work to do here and couldn't go with her. Not without worrying about her safety either, even though he knew that Megan could handle herself.

When the truck pulled back into the compound, late in the afternoon, he saw Ranjini hurry out to greet her. Then watched as Megan disappeared out of view, obviously making for her bungalow. Jaye finished his afternoon ward round and then went to his bungalow, fetching the bottle of brandy that he kept for emergencies along with a couple of glasses.

He found her sitting under the tree, as he'd known he would. When he put the bottle and glasses on the wicker table, she smiled up at him.

'So you want a full report on how it went?' She nodded at the bottle.

Jaye sat down, pouring a little of the brandy into each of the glasses. 'Yes. Four days' worth.'

She laughed. 'Okay. I'm glad to be back. Warmish water in the shower and a soft bed.'

'You could swap bungalows with me if you want hot.'

'No, I'll keep the one I have. Warm water's fine and I like the shade. Yours is too hot.'

Jaye leaned back in his seat, taking a sip from his glass. 'So what about the places you saw?'

Megan told him all about the sites they'd visited, people she'd met and places she'd seen. Jaye listened, as if he hadn't visited them himself, many times. She made it sound fresh and new.

'So you're going for the more central site.' It would have been his choice too.

She nodded. 'I think so. The existing facilities aren't as good, but that's something we can change. We want a location that's accessible to as many people as possible. And there's plenty of space there to build.'

Jaye smiled. 'You're thinking of building something?' Of course she was. Megan might content herself with the status quo, and make the best of it, but she never lost sight of the possibilities.

'I'm just saying that if the project is successful, there's space to build.' She grinned at him.

'Here's to it, then.' He refilled their glasses, clinking his against hers.

'Yeah. Even if I don't get to see it.'

If everything went to plan, she would. She'd be involved with all of the new developments that the charity was undertaking, all over the world.

'You're not thinking of going anywhere, are you?'

'No. But even the basic clinic's going to take a while to set up. I'll probably be gone by that time.' She looked at him thoughtfully. 'Wherever John Ferris decides to send me.'

This was the one thing he'd kept back from Megan. It

was *his* decision, not John's. She'd done well here, and he'd already emailed John to tell him that Megan should be offered the post that had been discussed when she'd been recruited. It was sooner than intended, but she was ready.

He'd kept quiet about that, though. The fragile balance of their relationship would be tipped if Megan felt that her future depended on his assessment of her.

'Well, here's to coming back.'

'Yes. It is beautiful here.'

Jaye smiled. Six weeks ago she hadn't yet had a chance to see the beauty of this country or to connect with its people. Now she'd used her growing connection with both to underpin her determination to give the right help, exactly where it was needed.

'It is. This place is something special.'

'Is that why you were so stressed out? When you got here and found that it had changed?' Megan deftly put her finger on one part of the reason, conveniently forgetting that she was another part of it. She must know that she had been.

'Yes. But it's built on good foundations, with good people. All it needed was a nudge to get it back on track. And now that it is, it's one of my favourite places in the world again.'

She smiled lazily. 'What is it you like best about it?'

One of those half serious, half playful games, played over a couple of drinks, to pass the time on a long, hot evening. Jaye could go for that.

'The people… And everything's less complicated here.'

She grinned at him. 'Is that because you've got a great big house at home to store your complications in while you're gone?'

'Probably.' Jaye chuckled. 'I love the silence just before the dawn. No old floorboards to creak around you.'

'You like being a doctor, don't you? More than you like being a duke.'

'Yes, I like being a doctor very much. I can't do much about being a duke, but it gives me the ability to do things I couldn't otherwise do.'

'Means to an end?'

'Sometimes…'

'And other times?'

He shrugged. 'People can look at you differently. In fact, they sometimes don't look at you at all, they're too busy looking at the house and everything that comes with the title.'

She was nodding slowly. 'Sonia?'

'Yes. Amongst others.'

'But here you're a doctor.'

Jaye nodded and they lapsed into companionable silence. Drinking buddies on a warm evening, who could just let the time slip by and the conversation go wherever it wanted.

'So how about you? Why did you want to become a nurse?'

'I didn't actually. I had to do something, though…'

'And the careers guide just happened to fall open at the letter N?'

Megan laughed. 'No, I chose nursing because my father wanted me to do business studies at college. He was going to take me into his company and fast-track me, without anyone knowing who I really was, of course. So I picked the course that I thought he'd most disapprove of.'

'Which was nursing.' Jaye chuckled. Megan had always seemed so sure of her goals, so focussed, and it was ironic that she'd fallen into the one thing that seemed to define her by accident.

'Yes. You're not taking notes, are you? I'd be devastated if this turned up on my employment file.'

'I don't need to take notes. I've got this place fitted with hidden cameras.'

'Oh, hidden cameras are okay. So, anyway, I started the course, with the idea of dropping out in six months' time and going travelling. But then I fell in love with the job.'

Jaye chuckled. 'So you were caught out by your own scheming.'

'Yeah. I was pretty immature in those days. Nursing knocked a lot of things out of me, and I'm lucky I found it before I did something stupid.'

'I…can't really imagine you doing something stupid.'

'No? I found out who my father was when I was thirteen. Before that I just thought he was an uncle. I spent a bit of time after that concentrating on doing as many stupid things as I could think of, just to annoy him.'

'That sounds…'

'Constructive. It was a very constructive reaction.' She turned the corners of her mouth down, giving the lie to her words.

'How about understandable, then? It must have been a bit of a shock.'

'Yes, it was a shock. He used to come and visit when I was little, and he'd bring me presents and take my mum and me out to nice places. When I found out that it was all a lie…it felt as if *I* was a lie. As if I had no real right to exist.'

Jaye's heart thumped. He wanted to reach out and comfort her but that wasn't what drinking buddies did. He picked the bottle up from the table, tipping another splash into both their glasses. She seemed to understand the meaning of the gesture, giving him a little nod before she took a sip.

'And nursing was your one big rebellion.'

'It is now. When I was a teenager I used to specialise

in unsuitable boyfriends.' She flashed him a grin that was pure mischief.

'You can't stop there. Unsuitable how?'

'Well, they weren't really unsuitable as far as I was concerned. Being unsuitable in my father's eyes was always a big plus point for me. One of them was a professional poet. He travelled around in a beat-up minibus, giving readings in the evenings and doing odd jobs to make ends meet during the day.' She laughed.

'And your father didn't like him.'

'He loathed him. The whole thing was a bit of a non-starter really, but the fact that Harry was purple with disapproval made me hang on in there for almost two years. I had a lot of fun, went to quite a few music festivals, and then we went our separate ways.'

'So you wouldn't mind if we put a few poetry books in the back of the medical truck? Did a few readings when we weren't otherwise occupied?'

She laughed. 'No. We're not doing that. I think that's enough skeletons in cupboards for this evening. What are your top ten favourite films?'

Megan rolled over in her bed, reaching for something. Someone. It took a few moments to slough off the remains of sleep and remember that Jaye wasn't there.

They'd talked for a long time last night. Favourite films, favourite books. Best music tracks had been a hard-fought one. Jaye preferred jazz and she liked rock. And lubricated by a long day, a dark evening and more than one measure of brandy, they'd both probably said far more than they'd intended about themselves.

And when finally he'd propelled her towards her bungalow, both stumbling and laughing quietly in the darkness, he'd lingered for a few moments on the porch. So close that Megan had found herself melting at the thought of a goodnight kiss.

But she hadn't been *that* drunk. If the darkness would cover anything they did, if Jaye's sense of discretion could be relied on to keep it away from anyone here, it would still have been a secret. And Megan wasn't like her mother. She didn't do secret relationships, and she didn't do relationships with her boss.

The banging on the door made her jump. It was far too loud to be Jaye, he would have knocked. Megan crawled out of bed, disentangling herself from the mosquito net and grabbing her dressing gown, and headed blearily for the door.

'We have many people for clinic today.' One of the junior nurses stood on the porch. 'Dr Jayananda says no time for sleep.'

A faint remembrance of how they'd come so close to having no time for sleep once before drifted into her mind. Megan was sure he would have woken her himself then, and in quite a different way.

But this was… If it wasn't quite so delicious, she could live with that. A busy clinic was something she could share with Jaye, and feel that it was a worthwhile thing and not an exercise in doing all the things she'd sworn to herself that she'd never do.

'Thanks. Will you tell him I'll be there in fifteen minutes?' A lukewarm shower would do wonders in getting those thoughts out of her head. Which would start the day the way she meant to continue it.

Megan shone a little bit more each day. Jaye had known that she would be the person he wanted as the charity's overseas co-ordinator almost from the start. Seeing her do what needed to be done, picking up a spade as readily as a medical bag when the situation called for it, had confirmed him in that thought.

He'd spoken with John Ferris, and they'd agreed that John would offer her the new job when she returned to London after her three-month placement here. And then Jaye had fallen back into the comfortable routine of working with Megan, pretending that he wasn't quite a boss and she wasn't quite a friend.

But he hadn't reckoned on how hard she was finding it to leave here. Every day the sadness in her eyes seemed to grow, and he longed to tell her that she'd be back. Finally, he broke.

The lights were on in her bungalow, and he could see her shadow against the thin curtains in the living area. Megan was obviously still up and still working. Jaye tapped on the door, holding the folded offer letter in his other hand.

'Have you got a moment? There's something I want to discuss with you.' Her gaze flipped behind him in the direction of his open-air office. 'In private.'

'Yes, of course. Come in.' She stood back from the door and started to gather up the papers and maps that had been spread out on the sofa. 'Sit down…'

'It won't take a moment.' Jaye felt his hand tremble, and put it in his pocket. He hadn't realised how very much this meant to him. 'I've been talking with John Ferris and he's asked me to give you this.'

'An official letter…?' She grimaced at the headed notepaper. 'Is it ominous?'

'No, it's not ominous.' Jaye hadn't been sure quite why he had gone to these lengths to step back from this. Rather than just tell Megan, he'd typed out the letter and signed it on John's behalf. It occurred to him that if she turned the job down, it might not be such a personal rejection that way.

She read the letter through, flipping through the pages.

As she did so, a smile began to grow on her face. 'You're offering me… Overseas Development Co-ordinator?'

'Yes. Don't be fooled by the co-ordinator part. We're hoping that you'll have hands-on, day-to-day contact with patients. A practical assessment of their needs is what drives us.'

She nodded. 'So…pretty much what I've been doing here for the last month?'

'Not quite. You'll have more authority, and a number of different sites to cover. There's travelling involved, but it won't be just a whistle-stop tour and then back to London. We'll be expecting you to stay with the various projects for a few months and get acquainted with what really makes each of them tick. Then work up proposals with the various directors of each centre and report direct to John Ferris and the board of trustees.'

'It sounds…' She smiled suddenly, flushing pink and pressing the letter to her heart. 'This is the job of my dreams, Jaye.'

And the quiver in his stomach wouldn't let up until he had a yes from her. 'And…?'

Suddenly she stepped forward, flinging her arms around his neck, and burying her face in his shoulder. It so surprised Jaye that he wasn't sure what to do, other than keep his hands hovering inches behind her back, not touching her.

As quickly as she'd done it, she backed off again, her cheeks bright red.

'What do you say, Megan?' He *had* to know. Now.

'Yes. Thank you, Jaye. It's what I really want. *More* than what I want. Thank you so much.'

'I can tell John that you've accepted the offer, then?' Jaye struggled to maintain his distance when all he really wanted to do was to hug her back and accept her thanks for himself.

'Yes. Should I write something?'

Probably not, since John would be expecting her to reply direct to Jaye. 'That's okay. I'll tell him, and you can sort out all the details when you get back to London.'

'And… Will I be working with you? From time to time?'

'Since I'm planning on spending more time here and with our other projects, I imagine our paths will cross fairly regularly. But we'll both be working quite independently of each other.' He saw Megan's cheeks burn hot again. If that was going to be a problem, then it was a big enough world, and he could contrive to avoid her. And he'd remind her that she'd already said yes and that he considered it binding.

'I'm so glad. I've seen what you've done here and it's… I really respect it.' She turned her gaze up to him, her eyes shining, and Jaye almost fell to his knees with a mixture of relief and sudden pleasure that she'd been taking notice and she approved.

'There's plenty more to do.' He risked a step further. 'I'm looking forward to tackling it with you.'

Megan was smiling now, a great big beautiful Cheshire cat smile, and as excitement set in, she could hardly keep still. She practically danced across to the small kitchenette, and Jaye watched her, allowing pleasure to seep into his bones.

'Coffee…? We have to celebrate, and this is the last I have left.'

Much as he would have loved to celebrate with her, in just about any way that Megan would let him, it was a bad idea. His own excitement and hers were an explosive mix, and Jaye already had what he wanted. He'd never forgive himself if he spoilt it all now.

'It's…a bit late for coffee.'

'You think I'm going to sleep? After this? Coffee's not going to make any difference. I can make you a cup of tea if you prefer it.'

'Thanks, but I need to turn in. But I'm really pleased you've said yes.' Jaye had reckoned on leaving the next bit for tomorrow, but he was on a roll. And he wouldn't be sleeping tonight either. 'There's one more thing. I want you to take a day off.'

Her eyebrows shot up. 'A day off? I don't have time. I'd set aside the next few weeks to finish up the plans for the women's centre with Ranjini.'

'You'll be coming back to do that. And you've been working twenty-four seven since you got here.'

Megan shrugged. 'Okay. I can…read a book, I suppose. Or sit under a tree.'

'And how long will you be able to keep that up for before you decide there's something pressing you need to do in the clinic?' Jaye grinned.

'A couple of hours. Possibly more.' Megan grinned back.

'That's what I thought. Which is why I have a proposal for you. I promised my parents I'd go up to their house here, to make sure it's okay. Since things are running pretty well now at the clinic, I have time to do it. It's thirty miles from here and we can be there and back in a day…' Jaye couldn't quite say the words.

Come with me. I want to spend the day with you.

'It's a long way to go just to make sure I take a day off.'

'If that's what it takes… Or I could lock you in your bungalow.'

'Nah. I'd find a way out.' Megan laughed. 'Okay, I'll come. Thank you.'

CHAPTER THIRTEEN

MEGAN HAD HARDLY expected the house to be anything other than beautiful. Set in the mountains, a little way back from the road, it was surrounded by lush trees, the roof sprawling out over a wide veranda that ran all around the building. It looked cool and serene after a hot and sticky drive.

Inside, the huge shaded windows, mosaic-tiled floors and pale walls gave the place an air of calm and quiet. White muslin curtains billowed lazily in the breeze, like flapping sails on a great ship, and the view across the mountains was spectacular.

'This is lovely, Jaye.' Despite the silence, the house was clearly regularly cleaned and aired. 'Is there anyone here?'

'The housekeeper and her husband. I've asked Mrs Jayasuna to make lunch but I have time to show you the garden before it's ready. Would you like to go upstairs and freshen up?'

He led her up the stairs to a large bedroom, dominated by a carved teak bed.

'You're going to tell me that this was all made in a little workshop that the charity sponsors, aren't you?' Taking an interest in the provenance of the furniture kept Megan's mind off the use to which the great bed could be put to.

Jaye chuckled, gravitating away from the bed and towards the table that stood by the window. Perhaps he was of the same mind, but somehow that didn't seem quite as challenging as it should be.

'Quite a big workshop, actually. And we don't sponsor them, they don't need it. But they do pay their craftsmen a fair wage and they only use sustainable timber.'

'For a better night's sleep?'

He grinned. 'Yes, much better. This was my parents' first home after they were married. When they got to the point of settling for long enough to have a home.'

'They travelled a lot?'

Jaye nodded. 'When you interviewed my parents, did my father tell you the story about pursuing my mother through five countries and two continents?'

'Yes. He went into some detail. He said that he met her here in Sri Lanka, while she was travelling. She didn't want to settle down, but he knew that she was the one for him. I thought that the five countries and two continents might be an exaggeration.'

'It's no exaggeration.'

'So she did play hard to get?' Megan couldn't imagine Jaye's parents ever having hesitated over making a commitment to each other. They seemed so right together.

'Not that hard. She always left a forwarding address. After a while, they decided that it was a lot easier to just travel together. Then they settled here and I was born.'

'Here? I didn't realise…'

'They came back to England to live when I was eighteen months old. I was born in this house.' He gave the bedroom one last look, and then turned quickly. 'I'll see you downstairs.'

Fifteen minutes later, Megan appeared on the veranda. She'd changed out of the chinos and blouse she'd travelled in and into a sleeveless blue dress that Jaye hadn't seen before. She looked lovely, and the thought that she'd done this just for him brought a lump to his throat. Maybe he should have dressed for the meal too, instead of just changing his shirt.

They had coffee on the veranda, and just to set the tone, Jaye brought up the subject of the women's centre. It was a delight to see Megan's eyes shine as they discussed the plans and delved more fully into the possibilities that she and Ranjini were hoping to make into realities. Then a turn around the gardens, stopping to identify trees and plants and to dangle their fingers in the shaded pool, where koi nibbled at their fingers and a grey heron eyed them beadily from its perch on one of the rocks at the centre of the pond.

Lunch was set out on the veranda. It was easy to keep talking because Megan was easy to talk to—always interested in the world around her. And talk warded off the silence, where nothing else lay but passion.

'You haven't played carrom, then?' Megan had asked him about the game that she'd seen Dinesh playing with one of the other men.

'No. Does it always involve shouting at one another?'

'No.' Jaye chuckled. 'The shouting's an optional extra. It's a bit like a combination between billiards and draughts.'

'Oh. Do you have a set here? Can you show me?'

Her glistening enthusiasm hovered in the air between them. Jaye fetched the polished carrom table, setting out the pieces and letting her choose one of the striker pieces from the box.

'This is so pretty.' She turned the heavy piece, inlaid with a carved flower, in her hand. 'What do I do with it?'

'Flick it with your finger, like this…' Jaye demonstrated with one of the other striker pieces. 'The idea is to get all nine of your pieces into the pockets at the corners of the board, and then the queen.' He indicated the red circular piece.

'Right. I've got it. I imagine there are tactics.'

'Of course. Concentrate on flipping the striker piece first.'

'So you're not going to employ your tactics first time around?' She shot him a reproving smile. 'Where's the fun in letting me win?'

'You think I'm going to let you win?' Jaye had reckoned on doing so for the first couple of rounds at least.

She flipped her striker piece carefully across the board. Not quite enough to make much of an impression on the cluster of pieces in the centre of the board, but not bad for a first try. Then she leaned back, folding her arms.

'Come on, then. Let's see how it's done.'

He won the first round, not as easily as he should have done, but Jaye laughingly declared himself out of practice. Megan's teasing encouraged him to try his best and win the second round more definitively. By the third round it had become a pitched battle.

'Uh…' Jaye winced as she deftly pocketed one of her own pieces. 'I'm going to have to watch your technique. Are you sure you're not an expert, and you're just suckering me in?'

'I play a decent game of bar billiards.' She grinned at him. 'And if I were suckering you in, you wouldn't know about it.'

'Think so? I'm not such an easy victim.' Jaye flipped his striker piece, missing the intended target completely.

'Ha! Sure you're not suckering *me* in?' Megan took her turn, pocketing the Queen, and Jaye totted up the scores.

'That's twenty-four points to sixteen.' He was still eight points in the lead, and the growing competitiveness between them made Jaye resolve to widen that gap in the next round.

'All right.' She rubbed her hands together, blowing on her fingers. 'Next round I'm going to take you down.'

He broke away with an effort, getting to his feet and walking back to the lunch table to retrieve the full bottle of wine they'd ignored over lunch in favour of sparkling water. Maybe a drink would stop his head spinning.

'I can see why you love this place so much.' Megan accepted the glass of wine with a nod of thanks. 'I wouldn't want to leave.'

'We always come back. When I was little, we used to come to Sri Lanka every summer. We caught up with our relatives on Dad's side, had a bit of a holiday, but my parents were already involved with some healthcare projects here.'

'As well as running the estate in Gloucestershire? It's a lot to do.'

'We have a lot of help to do it. My mother runs the estate when I'm away, but there are a whole army of people working there.'

'And you knew you'd be a duke? When you were a child?'

'Pretty much. My uncle died when I was nine, but he'd been ill for years before that, and he had no children. My mother and father never made too much of it but...' Jaye could still feel the sinking feeling when he'd been called into the headmaster's study the first term back at school after his uncle had died.

'Other people did?' Megan leaned forward in her chair, losing interest in the carrom table.

'The headmaster at my school told me that I was different. That I was going to have responsibilities and that I had to be prepared for them.'

'That's no kind of thing to tell a nine-year-old...' Outrage flashed in her eyes.

'Maybe. He was right, though. People treat you differently when you're a duke. It's the first thing they notice about you, and some people don't bother to look any further.'

She nodded, sitting back in her chair and sipping her drink. It seemed that she was content with just that, and Jaye felt a tenuous sadness that Megan was willing to accept the idea without some kind of protest.

'Is that what Sonia did?' Megan finally spoke.

'What makes you say that?' Even now, Jaye couldn't quite bring himself to admit it.

'Because… I was never that close to Sonia but whenever I did see her she was flashing that boulder you gave her. Was it real?'

Jaye snorted with laughter. 'Of course it was.'

'Just asking. I've never seen a diamond that big before. At least I can say for definite that I have now.'

She was teasing him, and Jaye didn't care. Suddenly, he could see Sonia from a different perspective. 'She was very pleased with it.'

'Tell me about it. It was all any of us heard about for months.'

'Well, she sold it after we split up. I heard from the jeweller who'd made it.'

The laughter drained from her eyes, leaving only tenderness. 'You let her keep the ring because you thought she might need the money. To bring up her baby.'

'Yeah. I had no use for it, and she… I loved her once.' It was as if the words no longer had the power to hurt him.

'That's a generous thing to do, Jaye. Really generous. Really crazy, too.'

'Yeah. I know.' Jaye leaned back in his seat staring out across the wooded hillside. 'I loved her, and she was in love with a piece of metal and rock and the idea of becoming a duchess. Story of my life.'

'It doesn't need to be. Can I ask…?'

'Ask me anything.' Suddenly none of this mattered. It was as if Megan had some wonder potion that she could sprinkle over him and take away all the hurt.

'Why did she call off the wedding? If she wanted to be a duchess so very much?'

'I'd been away in Sri Lanka for six weeks, a couple of months before the wedding, and when I found out that Sonia was pregnant… Well, the dates didn't make much sense. I asked her about it, and she admitted she'd had an affair while I was away.'

Megan was shaking her head. 'And to think that I believed you were to blame for it all. I'm so sorry, Jaye.'

'I didn't do anything to stop the rumours. I'd told Sonia that we could work things out, and that I'd adopt her child if that was what she wanted. She said she wanted to try, and we were going to counselling to get help. Then I found out that she was still sleeping with the father of her child. When I confronted her with it, she left me.'

'That's a vile thing to do. I'm so sorry it happened to you, Jaye.' Megan's eyes glistened suddenly with tears. The thought that she might shed just one tear for him and that he might be allowed to wipe it away left him breathless.

'She told me she'd never loved me. And I believe her, I don't think she ever did. She was always so in love with the idea of marrying a duke and being mistress of a big house. The thing that really cut me up was that she would have gone ahead and married me if I hadn't found out about the affair. It all meant that much to her.'

Megan shook her head. 'I always thought that Sonia was a bit silly, but… I didn't know she was that cold.'

'It's the way things are, Megan. It's who I am.'

'No, it isn't. It's the way *Sonia* was. It's nothing to do

with you.' Megan leapt to his defence so vehemently that Jaye could almost believe it.

A sudden clap of thunder made them both jump and rain began to fall, dribbling off the roof of the veranda. Megan shivered involuntarily, crossing her bare arms over her body.

'We should go inside. I need to find Mrs Jayasuna, there are a couple of things I need to ask her.' He could hardly tear himself away. Megan had just turned his world upside down. He'd told her his darkest secret, and suddenly it seemed just a thing that had happened. Too many years ago to be relevant now.

'I'll stay here if that's okay. I like watching the rain.'

He picked up a throw from the back of one of the wicker chairs further along the veranda and wrapped it around her shoulders. When Jaye's fingers grazed her cheek, she didn't flinch.

It could happen. The last time he'd touched her they'd both drawn back, but they trusted each other now. Jaye knew she wouldn't hurt him and hoped that Megan knew he would die before he hurt her.

'Thank you.' She turned her gaze up towards him, and he knew. He'd brought her here as a friend, hoping to give her a nice day out and some much-needed time off. But that friendship had finally broken the other barriers that lay between them. They would lead to a future which might hold anything.

They'd driven through the pouring rain and arrived back at the clinic just as it turned into a drizzle. Today had changed everything.

Megan could see it in his eyes. Dark and tender, like a lover's eyes. And after all this time, all the effort spent in trying to stay away from him, she finally believed that she might look into those eyes and surrender to them.

'Who's this…?' Jaye murmured the words as he turned into the compound, and Megan saw a large, black and chrome SUV, with tinted windows, parked outside. Dinesh was eyeing it from the shelter of the veranda, and one of the nurses was speaking to a man in a black T-shirt, which fitted tight across the muscles of his upper arms. Something about the way he carried himself said *bodyguard*.

Jaye stopped the car and swung down from the driver's seat. Megan followed him.

'Can we help you?' Jaye spoke to the man, and the nurse hurried away, obviously relieved that she didn't have to deal with him.

'This is the Western Province Free Clinic?' He had a trace of a cockney accent.

'Yes, it is.'

'I'm looking for Megan Wheeler.'

'That's me.' Megan stepped forward and Jaye laid his hand on her arm. There was something possessive about the gesture, which thrilled through her.

The man smiled at her. 'You have a visitor.'

Megan looked around him, trying to see who was sitting behind the car's tinted windows. It couldn't be…

'Who?'

The man was clearly not authorised to answer that question. He turned and jogged back to the car, reaching inside for an umbrella before his passenger stepped out into its shelter. Megan's heart thumped, almost painfully, in her chest.

No. Not here. Please, not now.

He was wearing a pale linen suit, creased by hours in the car. Blond hair, peppered with streaks of grey now. A few broken veins in his cheeks and a few extra pounds around the waist. But he was still imposing, looking around the compound as if he owned the place.

She wondered whether it might be possible to go and lock herself in her bungalow. But running away and leaving Jaye to greet him wasn't an option.

'Who's this?' Jaye was looking down at her with an air of troubled concern.

There was no point in telling Jaye that this was her uncle or a family friend. He'd see straight through the lie. And suddenly she wanted him to know.

'It's…my father.'

CHAPTER FOURTEEN

'MEGAN?' HARRY'S TONE implied that he was expecting some kind of welcome. When she didn't give it, he turned to Jaye.

'I'm Megan's uncle,' Harry lied smoothly, holding his hand out towards Jaye. 'I was just passing, and came to see what she's up to.'

Jaye shook Harry's hand, his face impassive. 'Pleased to meet you. You're very welcome here.'

'And you are?' Harry always liked to know whether the person he was talking to was worth his time.

'I'm sorry… Jaye Perera. I'm the clinic's director.'

Jaye never referred to himself as the director. He was happy with being the doctor, or peacemaker, or even temporary cook and bottle-washer if one was required. But he was on his guard, asserting his authority here.

'Is Mum all right?' A thought suddenly struck Megan and she blurted the words out.

'Your mother? She's fine. I called her last week and she told me you were here.'

When Megan thought about it, it wasn't very likely that Harry would come all the way here just to tell her that something had happened to her mother. And it was just like her mother to discuss what Megan was doing with Harry, even though Megan had asked her not to.

'She told you that I'd be back in London in a week?' She tried to dislodge the lump in her throat. When it came to the crunch, her mother's first loyalty was to Harry and Megan had to accept that. It was just one of the things that had driven her away from home as soon as she had been able to pack her things and go.

'Yes, she did. That's why I'm here now. There's something I want to talk to you about. And since I was on my way over to Australia on business I decided to stop off on the way.'

It was something of a detour. Whatever it was must be important, though Megan thought that it would turn out to be important to Harry and not to her.

'Aren't you going to ask me inside?' Harry smiled reproachfully, as if a welcome was something that might come naturally in this situation.

She supposed she should. Her bungalow was probably the best place to take Harry, so they could speak in private, but she hadn't allowed him admittance to anywhere she lived for a while now.

'Why don't you take my office?' Jaye spoke up suddenly, reaching into his pocket for the key. 'I'll rustle up some tea.'

'Thank you.' Harry beamed at Jaye again. 'I'm sure I wouldn't want to put you to any trouble—'

Jaye cut Harry short. 'It's no trouble. Is that all right with you, Megan?'

She looked up into his gaze. Warm and protective. If she asked Jaye to turn Harry off the compound, he would have done it, but just knowing he was there meant she didn't have to. Whatever had brought Harry here, she could face it.

'Yes, thank you. Everything's fine.'

'Okay. I'll see you later.' Jaye flashed another look at Harry, which seemed to threaten bodily harm if he put one toe out of line, and walked back to his car to fetch their bags.

'This way…' She started to walk along the veranda to the door that led to the offices, and then stopped. 'What about your driver?'

'He'll be all right in the car.' Harry looked up at the sky. 'Does it always rain like this here?'

'No. Not always.'

She'd let Harry into the office and pulled up two guest chairs. Harry had ignored them and walked around the desk, sitting in Jaye's high-backed chair.

'How have you been, Megan? It's been a while.' He leaned his elbows on the desk and smiled, for all the world as if he were interviewing her.

'Yes. It has.' Megan wasn't going to apologise for the length of time she'd managed to avoid seeing him. 'I'm well, and enjoying it here.'

'And working closely with Dr Perera, I see. Or does he prefer to use his title?'

Megan's heart sank. Of course Harry knew exactly what the set-up was here. He had staff to do almost everything for him, including keeping track of her.

'He prefers Dr Perera.'

'He's a good contact for you to make, Megan. That young man's making quite a name for himself.'

Harry was fishing. There was no way he could know how close she and Jaye had become as she'd told no one, not even her mother. Particularly not her mother, because things always seemed to filter back to Harry.

'He's a very good doctor. And a good boss, too.'

'I'm sure he is.' Harry beamed across at her. 'I always knew you'd come good in the end.'

Megan pressed her lips together, suppressing the urge to

tell him that there were some people who didn't think she'd totally wasted her life up till now, and that one of them happened to be Jaye. There wasn't any point, and it would be better if they got whatever Harry had to say over quickly.

'What are you here for, Harry?'

'You could call me *Father*.' Harry looked around the office. 'We're alone here.'

'We've been through that. If you want to keep it a secret that you're my father, that's fine. But if I can't acknowledge you in public, then I don't think it's appropriate for me to acknowledge you in private.'

Harry chuckled. It was always the first thing he did when Megan said anything he didn't much like. Pretend that it was just a laughable quirk on her part.

'I suppose *Dad*'s out of the question as well, then.'

She didn't have to take this any more. It was ten years since she'd called him *Dad* and then only under protest, because her mother had told her that they both depended on Harry, and that he could throw them out of the house they lived in on a whim.

'Yes. It's out of the question.'

The hurt look on Harry's face was no surprise. If he couldn't pretend that Megan was joking, he'd revert to the *What did I do to deserve that* look.

'It's a bitter pill for me to swallow, Megan. You're all I have now, and I haven't been well.'

The flash of concern she felt almost brought tears to Megan's eyes. She couldn't ignore this, however much she wanted Harry to just go away and leave her alone.

'What's the matter? Mum told me you'd had a pacemaker fitted six months ago but that you were doing really well.'

'It was eight months. And it's not right. I feel my heart thumping in my chest, and I'm sure there's something wrong.'

'Have you told your doctor?' Atrial fibrillation wasn't something that should be ignored.

'He doesn't take it seriously. He says my heart's fine, but...'

Megan reached forward, laying her fingers over the pulse in Harry's wrist. It was an automatic reaction, but the feeling that accompanied it was new to her. The feeling that Harry *couldn't* die.

'You care, Megan. No one else seems to.'

'That's not true, Harry, plenty of people care about you. So do I.' However unexpected it was, it was the truth. And Megan had resolved to always tell Harry the truth, however uncomfortable it might be.

Harry's heart followed the ticking of the second hand on her watch, a strong sixty per minute, regulated by the pacemaker. That didn't mean that he wasn't experiencing some irregularities, but it was something. Megan looked up at him.

'What's this all about, Harry?'

'My wife left me. The boys have taken her side... Ungrateful kids...'

'Like me? You always did say I was ungrateful.'

Harry puffed out a breath. 'You were a lot like I was when I was young. I went my own way.'

Her mother had always told her that she was like her father, that she had his eyes and his determination. Megan let out an exasperated breath.

'Harry... Look, I'm really sorry to hear that...there are obviously a lot of very stressful things happening at the moment.' Megan had never spoken about Harry's wife or sons, feeling that she had no right to even think about that part of his life. That she was the outsider, the child that should never have happened.

'She went off with someone else. Can you understand

how that makes me feel? She won't get a penny, my solicitor will see to that.'

'I can't… I can't talk about that with you. It's not right.'

'You were always the one, Megan. The boys are like their mother, but you've always been the one that was like me. Even when we argued, you were as stubborn as I am. I want you to come to Australia with me when I leave.'

A father. One that loved her. It was what Megan had always wanted, and Harry was dangling that prospect in front of her now. Of all the things he could have said, this was the cruellest. Megan blinked back tears, wondering what she could say to him. He was obviously upset and she couldn't help but feel for him.

A knock at the door made them both jump, and Harry snatched his arm back across the table. Megan could see a shadow behind the glass, and she got jerkily to her feet to open the door. Jaye was standing outside, holding a tray with cups and a teapot.

'You shouldn't have brought the tea yourself…' Harry's voice behind her. That was one trait Megan didn't share with him, she didn't have the ability to conceal her feelings at the drop of a hat. That mercurial switch that allowed Harry to declare complete love at one moment and then pretend he hardly knew you the next.

'The kitchen staff are busy.' Jaye walked past Megan into the room, and set the tray down on his desk.

He had meant to deliver the tea and leave. But one look at Megan's face changed Jaye's mind. He'd seen her angry before, and he'd seen her wrestling with a problem. He'd seen her covered in mud, hot and dusty and wet through. But he'd never seen her like this. She was so pale that her cheeks looked almost hollow, and her eyes were dull, almost as if she were in shock.

Jaye poured a cup of tea for Harry and put it in front of him on the desk. 'I'm sorry to intrude, but I wonder if I might borrow Megan for a couple of minutes.'

'Of course.' Harry seemed almost pleased with the idea. 'It's good to see that Megan's indispensable. Good people are...'

Jaye nodded. Good people *were* indispensable, but not when they were obviously so upset that they could hardly frame a sentence. Megan had opened her mouth and then closed it again, as if she couldn't find any words to say.

'Thank you. Back in a minute.' He bundled Megan out of the room, shutting the door behind them.

She looked around, as if she was unfamiliar with her surroundings. Jaye opened the door of Ranjini's office and, finding it empty, beckoned her inside.

'What's the matter, Megan? Is everything all right at home?'

'Fine.' Megan was standing by the door, her gaze fixed on the floor. 'Everything's fine.'

'But you're not.'

She shook her head.

If they were going to carry on like this, it was going to take a good deal longer than the couple of minutes he'd promised she'd be away for. And this sudden reticence was so unlike Megan that he knew something bad had happened. Jaye took her by the shoulders and she looked up at him.

'Megan, this isn't a game of twenty questions. What's the matter?' Perhaps he didn't have the right to ask. At this particular moment Jaye didn't care.

'Harry's... He wants me to...'

'What?' Jaye waited, not moving. They could work it out. They were good together, and they could do this.

'His wife's left him, and he says that he's not well. I

don't know if any of that's true but… He wants me to be his daughter.' A single tear rolled down her cheek. Tears would have been almost a relief at this moment, but her face was still inexpressive, as if she didn't dare feel anything.

'Let me help you with this.' Jaye could feel her slipping away from him.

She shook her head. 'I… You don't want to be mixed up with it. It's my problem.'

'We're friends, aren't we?' He'd dared to hope the future might bring something more, but right now a friend was what Megan most needed.

She looked up at him, her eyes wide and warm. 'Yes.'

'Then it's my problem too.'

CHAPTER FIFTEEN

SHE JUST WANTED Jaye to hold her. To tell her what to do. Harry had turned everything upside down, and she didn't know whether to hate him for it or run to his aid.

'Come here…' Jaye gently drew her close, and hugged her. She clung to his shirt, not sure how to respond, but his actions said everything. He was as steady as a rock and she could trust him.

'I don't know what to do, Jaye. I can't turn him away, he's in trouble. But he's up to something, he always is.'

'We can't turn him away at all now.' Jaye puffed out a breath. 'I saw the car turning in the compound and went out to speak to the driver. His instructions were to go as soon as Harry waved to him.'

Megan caught her breath. Harry had turned and waved to the driver as soon as she'd started to walk towards Jaye's office. 'He's gone?'

'Yes. It seems that Harry's intending to stay the night. Look, he's obviously got his own agenda here, and we don't know what that is. So I suggest you decide what you want to do and stick to it…'

'I don't know, Jaye. If this is just one of Harry's schemes to get what he wants, I won't give in to him. But suppose he really *is* in trouble. Suppose he's ill and needs my help. I can't turn him away.'

'Okay…okay. Let's think about this and take it one step at a time.' He drew back a little, motioning towards the two chairs that sat beside Ranjini's desk. Megan sat in one and Jaye in the other, leaning forward towards her.

'Harry says that he's not well. What's the matter with him?'

'He had a pacemaker fitted eight months ago. He says he's having palpitations. His pulse is normal, but that's no real indication….' Megan shrugged.

'All right. Think like a nurse. What's our guiding principle?'

Suddenly she knew. 'We treat everyone who comes to us, no fear and no favour.'

'And…?' He grinned suddenly.

'If someone says they have something wrong with them, we take that seriously and investigate. Even if we're not sure.' Megan couldn't help but smile back and Jaye nodded, brushing his fingers against her cheek.

'That's much better. So I'm going to insist on giving Harry the once-over. And before you tell me to back off and let you handle it, you're his daughter.'

'Biological daughter…' Megan wasn't sure she even knew *how* to be a daughter to Harry.

'Hey. It's okay to feel something, you know. And whatever you *do* feel is okay as well.'

It felt as if an enormous weight had been lifted from her chest. 'Thanks, Jaye.'

He got to his feet. 'It's what friends are for.'

It felt almost dizzying. Harry had always seemed so big, an irresistible force that she'd fought for so many years but had never quite got the better of. But with Jaye in the room he seemed smaller and much more compliant.

Jaye's charm persuaded Harry that a tour of the clinic

was what he most wanted to do next, and Megan plucked up the courage to mention that Harry should ask Jaye about the symptoms he'd been having. Harry brushed them off as nothing, and Jaye insisted. And then somehow Harry was walking towards Jaye's consulting room without any apparent protest.

When they reappeared they seemed to be sharing a joke together, and as Megan walked with them to the canteen, Harry asked questions about the clinic, which Jaye answered readily. Harry made no apology for dismissing his driver and effectively stranding himself here, and none was asked for. As darkness fell, she gave in to the inevitable and offered Harry her bungalow for the night.

As soon as the two men had shaken hands and Jaye had disappeared, Harry started to loom larger again. As she put freshly laundered sheets onto the bed, clearing her own things away into a drawer, he looked around the bungalow, shaking his head.

'You can do better than this, Megan.'

She felt fourteen years old again. 'It's good enough for me.'

'You don't need to settle for good enough. You don't have to give up your good works, it's something I respect you for. My company has a charity arm, for tax purposes. It would be a great deal more comfortable if you came with me and ran that.'

Megan sighed. Harry wasn't going to give up without a fight, and she just didn't have it in her tonight. 'We'll talk about it tomorrow, Harry. I've got some work to do.'

'At this time of night?'

'Yes. You'll be all right here?'

'I suppose I can make do.' Harry seemed to be able to shatter her world with just a few words. The little things that made her bungalow her own, the scent of fresh coffee and her candles, and the fabrics she'd used to brighten the place up, were nothing in his eyes.

'Goodnight, then. Don't forget the mosquito net when you go to bed.'

Jaye found her sitting in the corner of one of the wards, pretending to study a pile of patient notes. In reality, Megan was far too tired to read the words on the page in front of her, but she couldn't think of where else to go.

He sat down opposite her, and when Megan looked up at him, his face was expressionless in the shadows. Maybe he didn't see Harry quite the way she did.

'Have you gone over to the dark side, then?' She whispered the words so as not to disturb anyone.

Jaye smiled. 'Meeting Harry gave me a new perspective on why you don't mince your words. And, no, I haven't gone over to the dark side.'

'You seemed to be getting on pretty well with him.'

'And that's a problem for you? You don't have to justify the way you feel, Megan. If I thought it would solve anything, I'd be driving him back to Colombo right now.' His words were no more than a whisper, but they carried a hard edge of determination with them.

'You don't think that getting him away from here would solve *everything* for me?'

Jaye shook his head. 'No, I don't. Where are you sleeping tonight?'

Wherever she did sleep, it wasn't going to be under the same roof as Harry. 'I'll find somewhere. A bed in one of the side wards, where I won't disturb anyone...'

'They're all occupied. Dr Stone admitted a couple of new patients this afternoon.' Jaye got to his feet. 'Come on.'

'Where?'

'My bungalow.' He leaned down towards her, and Megan

shuddered, a tingle of excitement threading down her spine. 'You need some sleep.'

Jaye was the only person she could really trust. And Megan couldn't bring herself to care who saw them or what they might think. She rose quietly, stacking the patient notes back on the desk in the corner of the ward, and followed him.

Jaye had always wondered about Megan's father, and whether he was really as bad as she seemed to think. Now he knew that he was a great deal worse. Harry's observations during dinner, about Megan's childhood, and how proud he was of her, had seemed innocuous, but in the context of the truth he could see why they caused Megan so much pain.

'He said that you couldn't find anything wrong with him.' They dodged through the rain onto the back porch of his bungalow, and Jaye stopped to unlock the sliding doors. His bed still lay in disarray from where he'd left it in a hurry this morning, and he bundled her through to the sitting room, trying not to think about sleepless nights.

'That's a slight exaggeration.' Jaye flipped on the light and walked to the kitchenette. 'Everyone has *something* wrong with them, particularly as they grow older.'

She was smiling again. That was how he wanted to keep her. 'Okay, so you searched. What did you find?'

'His cholesterol's slightly high, which is a concern. I gave him some diet recommendations. And he admitted to rather more units of alcohol per week than I'd like to see.'

'That's not going to change.' Megan snorted with laughter. 'Harry likes a drink. What about his heart?'

'As far as I can gauge, his pacemaker's working as it should and his heart is healthy. But I've recommended that he gets a pacing check, sooner rather than later, and that will pick up any atrial fibrillation that's been going on.'

'We don't have that equipment here.' Megan shot him a querying look.

'Which is why I've been in touch with a contact of mine in Colombo and got him an appointment for tomorrow.'

Megan grinned suddenly. 'So you *are* sending him back.'

'No, I'm doing what needs to be done. I'd recommend exactly the same thing for anyone with a pacemaker who complained of irregularities in their heart rhythm.' He gave a shrug. 'I might not normally insist on a check the next day. But in this case…'

'Thank you.'

Jaye reached up into the cupboard, his hand hovering over the bottle at the back. Then he grabbed the herbal tea. They both needed clear heads for this conversation. 'Well, before you thank me, I was going to suggest that you make your peace with him before he leaves.'

'You don't know what you're asking.' Megan watched him drop the teabags into two mugs. 'Haven't you got any brandy?'

'Things are that bad?' Jaye reached for the bottle, and poured the smallest splash into a glass.

'He says that his wife has left him and that his two sons have cut him off. He's ill and he wants me to go with him to Australia when he leaves here, and then back to London to work with him. After all this time he's decided he wants me to be his daughter. He doesn't have anyone else.'

That did call for something stronger than tea. Jaye downed the contents of the glass, pouring another mouthful for Megan into a second glass.

'I don't know what to do, Jaye…' Tears formed in her eyes. 'I know that Harry's manipulative, and I take most of what he says with a pinch of salt. But suppose he really *is* ill and alone. Suppose he really does want to change.'

Jaye handed her the glass and sat down next to her on the sofa. 'You want to hear what I think?'

'Always. I have a feeling I might not like it, but at least it'll be the truth.'

The truth was the least he could give her. Even if his heart was banging in his chest and he wanted to be so much more than a friend in need.

'Harry treats you like a child. You say something he doesn't much like and he brushes it off or laughs, as if he knows better.'

Megan caught her breath. She'd always thought that, but hadn't dared say it. 'That's Harry…'

'No, it's not. He wasn't like that with me. It's how he tries to control you and put you down. You deserve a great deal more respect than that.'

'Is that supposed to be the part I'm not going to like?' Megan managed a smile, and Jaye longed to kiss the corner of her mouth. He made do with putting his arm around her shoulders.

'No, the part you're not going to like is that you need to stop accepting it from him. I think you need to decide what relationship you want with him and just tell him.'

'Easier said than done.'

'Of course it is. He *is* your father, and you want all the things that a father should give. But you may have to just accept that he's never going to be a proper father to you, and work with what you've got.'

She moved on the sofa, laying her head on his shoulder and hugging him. It was an exquisite form of torture, which Jaye wouldn't have missed for the world, because Megan needed someone. And being that someone was worth more to him than a dozen sleepless nights spent yearning for a more intimate touch.

'Thank you. I… I needed someone to say that to me.'

'Any time.' His throat felt suddenly hoarse and rasping. 'Sleep here tonight.'

'I don't think I'm going to sleep tonight. I might just as well stay on the ward...'

'You want to try something?'

Trust me. Say yes. Even though you don't know what I've got in mind.

'Okay...'

Jaye had instructed her to imagine a bubble around herself. Protecting her from everything. When Megan had wondered whether she might not float away, he'd grinned and added the image of a tree, its roots reaching deep into the earth.

'I'm that tree?' She opened one eye.

'Yes, you're the tree. You're strong and nothing can uproot you. And the bubble's there to stop you from being hurt. Close your eyes.'

'Okay. I don't think I need the bubble. The tree's good.'

'That's fine. Whatever works for you.'

'You do this a lot?'

'Every evening, I try to find some time to just...relax. Get a bit of balance.'

The Ayurveda. Jaye didn't practise Ayurvedic medicine, but it was everywhere here. And its principles had filtered into his life almost by osmosis.

'I don't think I'm very good at this. I'm still thinking...'

'Try this, then.' She felt his arm curl around her shoulders, and she melted into his warmth.

'Is this cheating?'

'No. I'm not teaching you to meditate, just trying to get you to relax. I think anything goes in these circumstances.'

She snuggled against him. 'Okay. In that case, I think it's working.'

CHAPTER SIXTEEN

IT WAS STILL dark when she woke, but the sound of birdsong told Megan that dawn wasn't very far away. For a moment she thought she was in her own bed, but then she heard Jaye moving quietly around in the next room.

Last night...

He'd held her and finally she'd gone to sleep in his arms. Megan had woken when he'd carried her into the bedroom, slipping off her shoes and laying her down. Then she'd felt him curl his body around hers, holding her. Nothing could touch her, not even Harry.

She was still wearing the loose shirt she'd had on last night, along with her underwear, but her chinos were folded neatly beside the bed. She sat up, listening for the sounds of Jaye's movements.

There was something odd about this. It took Megan a moment to gather her thoughts and realise what it was. *She* was always the first out of bed. Showering or making breakfast before a partner got the chance to get up. Being left behind was something that happened to her mother, not her.

She hadn't slept with Jaye. Or strictly speaking she *had* slept with him, but that was all they'd done. But the principle still held, didn't it?

Not this time, apparently. Megan didn't feel the usual

panic at finding herself alone in bed when the morning after dawned. She didn't need that element of control with Jaye because she trusted him.

The door opened quietly and then he appeared, showered and dressed in a loose white shirt and pair of well-worn jeans. Bearing coffee.

'You're awake?'

'Yes. And you're a marvel.' Megan pulled the mosquito net aside, reaching for the coffee.

Jaye watched the flickering light of the small torch he'd given Megan weave its way past the puddles on the gravel path that led to her bungalow. He missed her already. The feel of her body against his. The soft sound of her breathing in the darkness. He'd hardly slept at all, just lain awake, not questioning the feeling of complete happiness that had enveloped him.

He saw her briefly at breakfast, and then again as she and Harry walked through the trees at the far end of the compound, deep in conversation. He shouldn't interrupt. Megan needed to do this alone.

All the same, time dragged heavily on his hands. The clinic was operating smoothly now, and Ranjini and Dr Stone had built an easy working relationship based on mutual respect. No one needed him, as either a doctor or a peacemaker, and he retreated to his bungalow to sprawl on the sofa and watch the clock ticking.

A tap on the door roused him from the uneasy doze he'd fallen into. When he opened the door, Megan was standing outside, her cheeks flushed. Jaye stepped back from the doorway.

'Sit. Tell me how it all went.'

She plumped herself down on the sofa and Jaye sat next to her. For a moment she was silent, as if she was still working out how things *had* gone, and then she flashed him a smile.

'I told him that I wanted to help him but that I wasn't going to just drop everything and follow him. We talked about getting regular medical advice, and I suggested that he at least try and build some bridges with his wife and sons.'

'And how did he take that?'

'He said I didn't understand the complexities of the situation.' She shrugged. 'I seldom do, according to Harry.'

There was something different about Megan this morning. She seemed to be stepping back a bit from what Harry said about her and making up her own mind. It warmed Jaye's heart.

'So you told him you're not taking his job?'

'Of course I did. I never even considered it. It would have been a disaster...' She broke off, her hand flying to her mouth. 'You didn't think I was, did you?'

Jaye chuckled. 'Not really. If I'd thought it was a serious possibility, I'd have diagnosed Harry with an obscure tropical disease and had him put in isolation for a couple of months.'

'No, you wouldn't.' She paused for a moment, the idea of having Harry put into isolation for a couple of months clearly pleasing her. 'I told him I was happy with the job I have. That I have a promotion coming up and nothing's going to stop me from taking it.'

'Good for you.'

She nodded a wordless thank you. 'I told him that I wished him well, and that I hoped we could have a friendly relationship in the future. He has my email address and if he writes to me I'll write back. But no more turning up without warning and no more job offers. No more telling me what to do with my life either.'

Jaye smiled. 'What did Harry say to that?'

'Oh, he tried appealing to my better nature. Then he shouted a bit, because that's Harry. Then he told me that I was heading for disaster, and I'd end up with some kind of tropical illness and living on the poverty line.'

'Okay. I'm taking him back to Colombo now.' Jaye made to stand, but Megan caught his arm, pulling him back down.

'No, you're not. I told him to call his driver and he'll be here soon. He'll be back there in plenty of time for his appointment at the hospital.'

'Well, that's something. I'll call my colleague—'

'No, you're not doing that either. Harry's perfectly capable of telling him what he thinks is wrong with him.'

Jaye chuckled. 'Okay. Fair enough. So how do you feel now?'

Megan thought for a moment. 'It's all been a bit overwhelming. But I'm pleased that I've finally managed to deal with Harry on my own terms, because that's allowed me to contemplate having some kind of relationship with him. Not a proper father-daughter one but something. I owe that to you, Jaye, I couldn't have done it without your support.'

Her eyes were warm, with a hint of humour and a large helping of determination. Jaye looked into her gaze, feeling a strange giddy sensation, as if he were falling head over heels.

'What now?'

'Will you come and say goodbye with me?'

'Yes, of course.' He took her hand. 'Megan, this might not be the time to ask you…'

'Ask.' The look in her eyes urged him on.

'I'll leave a light out tonight. In case you want to know where I am.'

She smiled up at him. 'I'll find you.'

* * *

As luck would have it, almost as soon as they'd said good-bye to Harry, and Jaye had watched his car disappear out of the compound, Ranjini had called him in to see a patient. The man had been brought into the clinic with injuries from a traffic accident, where two vehicles on an otherwise completely clear road had somehow managed to smash into one another.

Jaye had stabilised him and then accompanied him down to the main hospital in Colombo. He arrived back at the clinic late in the evening, and tramped through the mud to his bungalow.

After all the nights that he'd welcomed the long hours, so that he didn't have to think too much about sleeping alone, he'd wanted tonight to be different. He threw his keys down onto the coffee table and walked through to the bedroom, surveying the rumpled bed. He'd meant to tidy up a bit in here, too.

He just hoped that Megan knew what he'd been doing. That she hadn't waited to see the light in his window, and wondered why it wasn't there.

Then he saw it. A flickering light, coming from the direction of Megan's bungalow. Jaye hurried to the sliding doors and pulled them back, feeling the cool kiss of rain on his face as he stared into the darkness.

Not caring that he was wet and probably looked as if he'd been dragged through a hedge backwards, he strode towards the light. He could see now that it was a candle, set on the windowsill, its flame beckoning him forward.

Almost as soon as he knocked on her door, she flung it open. She looked like an angel, dressed in a pretty white blouse, her blonde hair shimmering around her shoulders.

'Megan, I'm so sorry…'

'It's all right. I know where you've been.'

'I got back as soon as I could.' Just this one look at her was enough. He'd go back to his bungalow and dream of her all night.

She reached out, hooking her finger into the front of his shirt. 'Come here.'

'I'm all wet…' He didn't dare touch her. She was far too perfect.

'Then take it off.' She banged the door closed behind him.

The room was neat and tidy, as it always was, illuminated by the soft light of the candle. Jaye kicked his boots off, trying not to get mud on the floor.

'Megan, I…' She laid her finger across his lips. Then she curled her hand around the back of his neck, pulling him down to kiss him. Jaye gasped, aching to touch her but aware that his hands would leave smudges all over her blouse.

'I don't care, Jaye. You've done a hard day's work, but now you're here.'

'You'll take me like this?'

'This is just the way I want you.'

He gave in. Pulling her close, he kissed her, feeling her soft warmth radiating through him. She dragged his shirt from his shoulders, dropping it onto the floor. Then she led him through to the bedroom, switching on a lamp beside the bed and opening the door to the tiny shower room.

After making quick work of their clothes, Jaye soon discovered that although soap and warmish water were unlikely aphrodisiacs, Megan made them work. He revelled in her touch as she washed him clean, crushed up against him in the cramped space. Jaye towelled her dry, then picked her up, carrying her the few steps over to the bed.

'Mosquito net…' She grabbed at the net and missed it. Jaye settled her onto the bed, pulling the fabric down around it. Their own small refuge, which provided everything he needed and wanted.

'You are so beautiful...' He sat opposite her on the bed, kissing the tips of her fingers, one by one.

She smiled up at him. 'It's taken us a while to get here.'

'It was worth the wait. Every moment of it.'

She liked it that he was a little shy, a little hesitant when he first touched her. As if the man beneath all the trappings of his position and wealth didn't take it for granted that she might want him.

Telling him how much she *did* want him, feeling his body respond to her words, was the most exquisite pleasure. And when he did touch her, he knew exactly what to do.

'Closer....' He whispered the word, his arm curled tight around her waist as he gripped her ankle, pulling it behind him. Tangled together, each caress thrilling through her body.

And then closer still. Pulled into his embrace, moulded against his strong frame. Still face to face, their arms and legs wrapped around each other. Jaye took every moment, fashioning it into something special.

'Closer, Jaye.' The one thing she wanted now was to have him inside her. She reached for the condoms she'd tucked under her pillow and pressed one into his hand.

No fuss, just a slight pulling away, which meant nothing because their gazes were still locked together in an unbreakable embrace. Then he leaned back against the head of the bed, lifting her onto his lap. Trapped again in his arms, all she could do was feel, as he slid gently inside her, smothering her gasps with kisses.

'Comfortable?' Jaye was a tender lover, and it was no surprise that he hadn't left his manners behind, tangled with his clothes on the floor. His gaze was always on her face, every caress guided by her reactions.

'Very…' She gasped the word and he smiled.

'Move for me. Show me all the things you want…'

No man had ever treated her like this, made her feel as if everything he did was for her. It was overwhelming, and Megan was dimly aware that he'd taken something from her. His tenderness, his attentiveness to her needs had ripped away her self-control.

She moved against him, feeling the warm sensation tingle through her veins. When he touched her again, she began to tremble.

His caress was no longer something that she wanted but something she needed. Finally, he laid her down on the bed, coaxing the orgasm out of her as if it were something very precious to him. The feeling tore through her, unstoppable and unchangeable. Pure release.

Then suddenly he too lost control. His movements quickened and a low gasp was wrenched from his lips. Finally, *finally,* Jaye was taking what he wanted. It felt like the ultimate surrender on his part.

'Megan…' It seemed almost like a cry for help.

'I've got you.' She held onto him, feeling sweat rise on his back as his body stiffened and convulsed. He let out a groan and she felt him pulse within her. Deep and strong, as if his own release could touch her heart and set it beating to his rhythm.

They clung to each other, sheltering in the silence after the storm. Then he moved, kissing her forehead, curling his body around hers in an obvious invitation to sleep. Suddenly all she wanted to do was to share this with him too.

'You'll wake me?'

'I'll wake you.' He kissed the top of her head. 'If you don't wake me first.'

Megan snuggled against him. She could dream for a while and then let her dreams melt into reality.

* * *

Jaye watched her drift off to sleep. It was a last acknowl-edgement of trust, the way she allowed him to hold her while she slept, knowing that he'd be careful to bring her pleasure when they woke.

He *was* always careful. He was a lover with something to prove, never sure whether his partners saw him as part of a greater package, and wanting some proof that they accepted him as a man. But there could be no question about whether Megan wanted him or not. She'd torn away all his self-doubt, and left him naked.

He waited, wondering how long he could stay awake, wanting to waste nothing of the night. But the warm relaxation was too much for him and he began to doze:

Megan's wake-up call was worth every moment she'd squandered in sleep.

'Are you still asleep?'

'No…' He stretched his arms, reaching for her, but she wasn't there. Just her voice, drifting through his consciousness like a siren's call.

'Sure?' He felt her fingers brush the top of his leg. Jaye's eyes snapped open suddenly, and he blinked in the soft light of the lamp beside the bed.

'Very sure. Megan, what…?' He groaned as he felt her fingers exploring. The feel of her lips against his skin. Arousal shot through his body.

He couldn't see what she was doing, but he could definitely feel it. It was all he could feel. 'Megan…' He choked out her name.

She fought her way free of the sheet that covered them, sitting up. She looked so beautiful, her blonde hair mussed around her head, her blue eyes shining with mischief. And she was completely naked. Jaye bent one leg, and she leaned against it, propping her elbow on his knee.

'Come here.' He wanted to make love to her again. To be the man that she wanted.

Megan shook her head. 'This time it's all for you.'

The small hairs at the back of his neck prickled. *That* was a more risky proposition.

'Ladies first...' It was a given thing. He should show her that he wasn't the kind of man who expected everything to be about him.

'We've done that already.' She glanced downwards. Even her gaze had the power to arouse him, and Jaye bit back a groan.

She ran her fingers down his leg. Slowly, but the look in her eyes told Jaye exactly where she was headed.

Sweet, languid delight melted into roaring need. When finally she reached for the condom, rolling it down over him, he tried to move but she pushed him back down again.

'Oh, no, you don't.' She smiled down at him in gentle reproof. 'This is for *you.*'

She climbed astride him, and he was powerless to stop her. He came almost as soon as he was inside her, a shattering rush, which left no space for regret. And when she leaned down to kiss him, her lips tender, he realised she'd just taught him a lesson he'd never be able to forget. How to accept the gift of pleasure.

But it couldn't end there. Jaye wanted her even more than he'd done at the start, and even if he was incapable of putting that into practice for a while, Megan didn't seem to mind. She held him, and when they were both ready, they made love again.

This time, they were truly making love together. No touch was all for him, or all for her. There was no longer any such thing as giving or taking. Everything was about both of them, and when they finally slept, Jaye could imagine that she dreamed the same dreams as he did.

CHAPTER SEVENTEEN

HE KISSED HER and then left at six in the morning. Slipping out of Megan's bungalow, Jaye jogged across to his own and collapsed onto the bed.

As he'd pulled on his clothes, she'd watched. And as he'd bent to kiss her, she'd whispered in his ear, 'The best night of my life.'

It had been the best night of his life too. Jaye closed his eyes. He could still get another couple of hours' sleep, and he was going to need them. Because tonight they would do it all over again.

Jaye hadn't seen Megan all day as she was closeted with Ranjini, putting the finishing touches to the plans for the women's centre. But he knew she'd come to him. He spent an hour tidying up and then drew back the curtains, leaving the lamp burning. Ten minutes later he heard a knock at the door.

She'd been crying. He ushered her inside and she sat down, perching on the edge of the sofa.

'What's the matter, Megan?'

'Someone saw you…this morning.'

The tiny hairs at the back of his neck suddenly stood to attention. This was too soon. It was still something for them alone, and not for anyone else to know about just yet.

'Who?'

'One of the nurses on the night shift. She'd gone outside to have a cigarette.'

Jaye shook his head. 'Well, she shouldn't have been out there in the first place. I'll have a word with Ranjini…'

Megan flushed red suddenly. 'No, don't. She didn't do anything wrong, she was on her break.'

'She shouldn't have been smoking, Megan.'

'That's her affair. We're not the health police.'

'Okay…okay.' Jaye started to pace. 'I'll speak to her myself, then, and ask her to keep quiet. How did you find out? It's not common knowledge yet, is it?'

Megan was staring at him. As if her worst nightmare had just reared up and smacked her in the face. 'No, it's not common knowledge. She came to me herself and asked me if I was all right. She thought I'd been ill in the night.'

A quiet voice at the back of his head started to whisper a warning. Jaye tried to ignore it and the volume rose to a scream. 'What did you say?'

'I lied. I told her that I'd had a dose of food poisoning but that you'd come and I was okay.'

The sense of relief was short-lived. Megan had lied. Jaye knew exactly how she felt about that. It was an effort to still himself, but he needed to be calm. He sat down next to her, taking her hands between his.

'I know you hate it, Megan. But it was for the best.'

'So this is a secret, then.' Her face was expressionless.

'No, it's not a secret. It's just no one else's business but our own.'

Megan shook her head. 'That's not true, Jaye. You're the director and you can't be seen to be having an affair with one of the clinic staff. People talk, and they start to think that you're not as impartial as you're supposed to be. It undermines your authority, and that damages the clinic.'

He couldn't deny it. Didn't dare, because Megan would know that he was lying. 'Yes. That's true. Just give it a little time, Megan. When we know where this is going and we're ready to share then we can go public with it.'

'And in the meantime? We sneak around, and hope no one else finds out?'

The flat, emotionless tone of her voice was hurting as much as her words. Jaye got to his feet and started pacing again, unable to contain the clamour of conflicting emotions.

'What do you want me to do? We're not doing anything wrong, we just need to be a little discreet for a while. Until we're a little more sure.'

'I am sure.' Her voice was suddenly little more than a whisper.

'How can you be? Last night was… It was beyond words. But it was just one night.' Fear tore at him. Megan could break his heart in a way that Sonia had never been able to. He would risk that, but not in public. Not for everyone to see and know about.

Megan was twisting her hands in her lap, staring at her feet. 'Then we have to stop.'

'Why? Just because you can't see that I'm not like your father? Do you honestly think that's any different from thinking that the most important thing about me is that I'm Lord Marlowe or that I have a big house? I want you to see me as I am.'

Something that had been precious to him was crumbling before Jaye's eyes, tainted with a poison that existed only in Megan's mind. He could forgive her anything else, but not this.

'I can't do it. Not even for you, Jaye.'

When she got to her feet, he knew she was leaving and didn't even want to stop her. That was the cruellest blow of all. Jaye turned, striding into the bedroom and slamming the door behind him. Megan could go if she wanted to, but he wouldn't watch her do it.

Megan undressed slowly, carefully folding her clothes. Cleaned off her make-up and smoothed in a little moisturiser, as if this determined bedtime routine might somehow get her in the mood for sleep.

But plumping the pillows and arranging them just as she wanted them, before pulling back the covers, wasn't fooling anyone. The moment his lips had touched hers, she'd known it. She loved Jaye.

Perhaps she'd known it all along. Megan turned the idea over in her head as she climbed into bed, switching the light off. It seemed now that she'd loved him all her life, that her tumultuous teens had just been because she'd been waiting for Jaye and had somehow known that she would have to wait too many years before she met him. As if defying Harry to become a nurse and finding her vocation in life had just been the first steps on the long road that had led to Jaye. Going to Africa, seeing the job with Jaye's charity in the paper... Navigating all the bends in the road, the crossroads and the dead ends to find him.

If that were true, it had been a wasted journey. The treasure at the end of the rainbow was fools' gold—a bright counterfeit. Because she and Jaye couldn't make it work.

She felt tears fill her eyes and blinked them away. The worst thing about it was that it was no one's fault. He needed time before he could bring himself to trust that she really loved him. But it was time that Megan couldn't give him, because every day she kept the secret would eat away at her and destroy what they had together.

Thunder rumbled, far away in the hills. Then came the

sound of rain on the roof of the bungalow. Megan turned over in bed, covering her head with her pillow. She'd never felt more alone.

By the time she'd got out of bed and dragged herself across to the canteen for breakfast, Jaye had gone. On the road somewhere, on his way to one of the villages and a patient he absolutely must see today. He got back late in the evening, and Megan saw the lights in his bungalow flip on briefly and then off again.

This wasn't going to blow over. She'd always be looking over her shoulder, bumping into him in every part of the world as part of her work. How many times had she wished that her mother would just give up on Harry, recognise that she could never have him and move on?

Her mother had ruined her own life, and Megan could take a lesson from that. As the dark, lonely hours of the evening dragged into a darker, lonelier night, she made her decision. And somehow even that heartbreak was comforting because she knew that there would be an end to it.

Megan looked tired this morning. Jaye had spent the last two nights missing her, and the intervening day working as hard as he could to drive away the memories of her touch. It had exhausted him, and it seemed that whatever Megan felt had exhausted her too.

'I want to talk to you.' She sat down opposite him as he sipped his third cup of coffee in the canteen. Maybe the caffeine buzz was what made her words sound so ominous.

'We can borrow Ranjini's office, she won't be in for another hour.'

She nodded, silently following him out of the canteen. Jaye knew exactly what he wanted to say to her. He'd rehearsed it enough times.

He sat down next to her in one of the chairs that Ranjini kept for visitors. 'May I say something first?'

Megan gave him the ghost of a smile. 'Yes, of course.'

Jaye took a deep breath. 'I'm sorry, Megan. I've thought about this a lot, and I know we have to end our relationship, but I don't want us to be on bad terms.'

'That's how I feel, too.'

'We've made a good start, then.'

'Yes. I've been thinking very carefully about…the job you've offered me.'

A sliver of alarm inserted itself in Jaye's heart. The thought that Megan might be about to do something stupid froze him, because there was absolutely no way he could stop her.

'Yes?'

'I've thought about all my options very carefully, and decided that it's…not appropriate. I'm sorry to mess you around but I won't be taking the job.'

Not appropriate. How many times had he used that term himself to soften things, to imply that there was no blame on anyone's part. The hypocrisy of it came back and slapped Jaye in the face.

'May I ask why?' Shock blocked all the things he really wanted to say and kept him still in his seat.

'I… I'm very sure about this decision. Please just accept that.'

He wanted to spring from his seat, take her by the shoulders and shake her. That was unlikely to go down terribly well, particularly since he'd just expressed the wish to stay on good terms with her, but he wouldn't let her go without putting up some kind of fight.

'Do you have another job?'

She shook her head. 'No.'

'You won't consider staying until you get something

else?' At least that would give him some time to try and change her mind.

'I don't think that's a good idea.' She attempted a smile. 'I won't be unemployed for long. If the worst comes to the worst, then I can always take Harry up on his offer.'

'No!' The word exploded through Jaye's reserve. 'I meant... Please tell me you're not serious about that.'

Tears welled in her eyes, and one dribbled down her cheek before she could catch it and brush it away. 'No, I'm not serious. You showed me how to stop compromising where Harry's concerned.'

And she wasn't going to compromise about this either. Jaye made one last-ditch attempt to hang onto something that he knew was already gone.

'Well, I guess... You're flying back to London in three days. Why not speak with John Ferris? I understand if you don't want to work with me. I can talk to John and we'll facilitate that.'

'Please, Jaye. Just let me go. It's the one thing you can do for me.' She turned her gaze onto his face and he felt a shimmer of warmth. Jaye knew that he couldn't bring himself to hurt her any more.

'Then... I respect your decision. If there's ever anything I can do...'

'Thank you. I'd be grateful if you could organise a reference for me.'

'Yes, of course.' He'd write a reference that would get her any job she wanted. And get John to write one too. 'I'll see you again before you go?'

'Maybe. We'll take that as it comes, shall we?'

Suddenly he didn't want to see her again. The sooner she left, the sooner he could beat himself up over taking the best thing that had ever happened to him and destroying it.

Megan got to her feet, and he automatically rose, opening the door of the office for her.

As soon as she was gone he started to pace, measuring the length of the room with his strides. The worst thing about all of this was that Megan was right. Ending something that was never going to work was the right thing to do, and Megan had been braver than he was. She'd given up the job of her dreams to do it, and the least he could do was support her in that.

Jaye had driven down to Colombo, and wasn't expected back for four days. Ranjini had given Megan the news gently, her quiet eyes seeming to understand that something was up.

The relief of knowing that Jaye was gone finally allowed her to sleep a little that night. Ranjini had insisted that she take the next few days off so she could pack and get ready to leave, and Megan spent them in a blur of numb misery.

Finally, it was time to go. Megan was up at five in the morning and ready to leave a half hour later. Ranjini was there to wave her off, dropping a beautifully wrapped package into her lap when she got into the car and telling her not to open it until she got back home to London. Dinesh delivered her smoothly to the airport, carrying her bag for her to the queue at the check-in desk. Megan bade him a warm goodbye, insisting that he didn't wait to see her through.

The first day of the rest of her life. It hurt, but Megan knew it was the right thing to do. She could get over this, starting now, and live her life the way that her mother had never had the courage to live hers.

The queue moved slowly and finally she reached the desk. The gates were ahead of her, and when she got through she'd be able to breathe again.

'Megan.'

She felt a light touch on her arm, and shrank away from it. No.

'Megan…' This time Jaye's voice was a little louder. A little more insistent. Ignoring him wasn't going to make him disappear so she turned to face him.

'I'm next up…'

'No, you're not.' He turned to the woman behind the desk, giving her the full force of his smile. Murmuring an apology, he stretched over and lifted her bag off the conveyor belt. Then he took Megan's arm, guiding her away.

'No… Jaye!' She tried to pull away from him but his fingers tightened. This wasn't Jaye. She was being kidnapped by a lookalike. 'Look, I've lost my place now. I'm going to have to queue all over again.'

'Yes, you are.' Jaye's immaculate self-possession had slipped, and there was something boyish about him.

'Let me go, Jaye.' There was no way that a man like him could ignore that.

He let her go, but only so that he could grab the ticket and her passport from her hand. Then he turned, pushing through the people hurrying past them, making for a quiet corner.

'Jaye. Don't you dare do this. Give me my passport back…' Megan didn't have much choice but to follow him. If he'd just walked off with her luggage, she would have thought seriously about getting on the plane without it, but without her passport and ticket she was stuck.

'In a minute.' He came to a halt, putting her bag down at his feet.

'No, now. Or I'll call Security.'

'Go on, then. My Sinhalese is better than yours.'

'This is an airport. I dare say they'll understand "This man's bothering me".' The idea of being labelled as the kind of man who bothered a woman had to be about the worst thing possible in Jaye's book.

'And then they'll probably arrest me. Or you could give me five minutes of your time.'

'It doesn't take five minutes to say goodbye.' Megan spread her hands in an expression of frustration. 'There. Goodbye. That's it. Now give me my passport or I will call Security.'

'You want to see me in jail?'

'Right now it might be the best place for you. What's got into you, Jaye?'

'Nothing. Something's been driven out of me.'

He did look different. As if a burden had been lifted from him. Maybe he was relieved that she was going and he'd come to twist the knife in the wound by telling her so.

But, whatever else he was, Jaye wasn't cruel. He wasn't making any sense either, but if he just wanted five minutes, she could do that, if it meant that she could get her things back and go without the need for him to be incarcerated.

'All right. Five minutes.' She glanced at her watch in a clear signal that she was timing it. 'Then you give me my passport back.'

He nodded, taking a deep breath as if preparing for something. 'Megan, I can't let you go without telling you...'

Megan closed her eyes. This was going to be worse than she'd thought. But it was five minutes and then she'd be through to the passenger lounge and out of his reach.

She felt his touch on her arm, suddenly tender. Her eyes snapped open. 'You can't let me go without telling me what?'

'That I love you. And asking you to give me another chance.'

'We've used up all our chances, Jaye. They didn't work out...'

'Because I couldn't trust enough. I didn't believe that you could possibly love me for myself, and so I threw it all away. But I want it back. No more discretion, no more lies. I'm in love with you and I want everyone to know it.'

She stared at him. His eyes were soft, his face more handsome than any man she'd ever seen, and bright with the promise of someone who was starting afresh.

'I... You have my passport.'

His gaze never left hers as he pressed her ticket and passport into her hand, sliding her bag towards her with his foot. 'Here. Take it and walk away.'

She couldn't. 'Are you saying...that you wouldn't try to stop me?'

'I wouldn't stop you. I might follow you, though. It's a bit of a family tradition.' His fingertips traced down her arm. 'If we weren't in public, I'd kiss you now.'

'We'd get into a lot of trouble. The way I'd be kissing you back...' In the heat of his gaze it felt almost as if he *were* kissing her.

His lips curved into a smile. 'Yeah? Think you can hold that thought?'

'I'm holding it. Tight...' Heat was building between them, spiced by longing and the knowledge that if they did any more than just hold hands, Jaye would most probably have airport Security tapping on his shoulder.

'I love you, Megan. And if you love me back then it's going to tip both our worlds upside down. We'll both have to re-evaluate all the things we've believed about ourselves for a long time now. But we both have the power to do anything we want, if we'll only take it.'

'My world's already tipping.' She rubbed her finger gently against his wrist, and saw his eyes darken. Less really was more.

'Mine too.' His fingers closed around hers and Megan stifled a gasp. 'If you follow me now, I'll follow you, wherever you want to go.'

'Five countries? Two continents?'

He nodded slowly. 'That sounds just about right.'

She smiled up at him. 'Wherever you are is my home, Jaye. What do you say I follow you? I'm sure John Ferris has plans for you.'

'We can work that out, Megan. We'll follow each other.'

'Okay. All I want is four walls and enough privacy to kiss you and take off your clothes…'

'You think I'm not naked now?' His lips curved in a delicious smile.

In everything other than actuality, they were. More naked than they'd ever been together, closer and more at one, even though only their fingers were touching.

Wordlessly he picked up her bag, slinging it over his shoulder. Megan stowed her passport and the wasted ticket in her handbag. Then he took her hand, leading her away.

EPILOGUE

FIVE COUNTRIES AND two continents. That was if Jaye managed to get through customs.

He'd told Megan to go on ahead, through the 'Nothing to Declare' channel, and he'd catch up with her. After a long flight from Indonesia to Melbourne this was the last thing they needed.

She stopped, keeping him in view, as he talked with the customs officer at the desk. The conversation seemed to be friendly enough, but the man wasn't letting Jaye go.

'Just keep going, miss. Through the door over there.' A woman officer was directing people through the doors once they'd been through Passport Control.

'I'm waiting for my partner. They've stopped him and I don't know why…'

'I'll go and see.' The woman officer walked over to where Jaye was standing, and he spoke briefly to her. She nodded and walked back to Megan.

'Everything's okay, we just need a form filled out. Go and wait outside, he won't be a minute.'

'But…' The woman ignored Megan's protests, and smilingly shrugged when she asked what it was that required the filling out of a form, shepherding her towards the doors.

Okay. So she'd go through the doors but she wasn't letting Jaye out of her sight. Megan stepped to one side, pressing her face against the full-height glass so that she could see him. But he was following the customs officer through a door into what must be an interview room.

She waited for ten minutes. Then ducked back inside and marched up to the woman she'd spoken to. 'Please, can you tell me what's going on? Is there something that I can help with?'

'No. You should wait…' At that moment the door that Jaye had disappeared through opened, and he emerged. Striding up to her, he put his arm around her shoulder, smiling at the woman officer and guiding Megan away.

'What was that all about?'

Jaye walked through the doors and stopped suddenly. 'This is the fifth country. And the second continent.'

'I know.' Jaye had been uncharacteristically tight-lipped about their accommodation for tonight. And Megan's impatient hopes had been tempered by trust. Jaye would do the right thing, at the right time.

He took her bag from her hand and put it on the ground next to his. 'I'd planned this differently, but I can't wait…'

She knew, from the look in his eyes, what he was talking about. 'I love it that you can't wait. Neither can I.'

He dropped to one knee in front of her. 'I'll have your answer, then.'

'I'll have your question first.' Megan smiled down at him, her heart thumping. She so wanted to hear the words.

'Will you marry me, Megan?'

Just a few seconds, which would change her life for good. Megan was trembling, almost crying with happiness.

'Yes, Jaye.'

'You're sure?' He was teasing now, a broad smile on his

face. 'You don't want to think about it? It's a lot to take on. There's a title, and a house…'

'I'll take *you,* Jaye. The rest is just incidental.'

He took her hand and kissed it. 'I have a ring. It's what all the form-filling was about…'

She could only see a blurred flash through her tears. But she felt the band slide onto her finger, like an absolute bond that could never be broken. When he got to his feet, kissing away her tears, she saw all the promise of the years ahead in his eyes.

'You like it?'

She looked down at her hand. A pale blue sapphire, flanked on either side by two weighty diamonds. 'It's beautiful. Thank you, Jaye.'

He wound his arms around her shoulders and she clung to him. 'I really wish you'd stop crying…'

'Happiness, Jaye. You're going to have to get used to it.'

'I suppose I will. Because it's my job to make you happy now, and I intend to do it well.'

Megan laughed against his chest. 'Consider yourself employed. No trial period.'

He kissed her, and a loud whoop sounded from inside the airport building. When Megan looked round, she saw the two customs officers behind the glass, both waving and smiling.

'They knew?' She grinned up at Jaye.

'I didn't know myself until I was on my knees. I was going to wait until tonight to wine and dine you…'

'This was so much better. No champagne or beautiful rooms. Just you.'

'Really?'

Megan grinned. 'I'll take the champagne and the beautiful room later.'

He took her hand. 'Coming right up, Milady.'

'Oh, no. None of this "Milady" business. It doesn't suit me.'

He chuckled, brushing another kiss onto her lips. 'Too bad. You're going to have to get used to it.'

* * * * *

If you enjoyed this story,
check out these other great reads from
Annie Claydon

SAVING BABY AMY
ENGLISH ROSE FOR THE SICILIAN DOC
THE DOCTOR'S DIAMOND PROPOSAL
RESCUED BY DR RAFE

All available now!

TEMPTED BY
DR OFF-LIMITS

BY
CHARLOTTE HAWKES

Published in Great Britain 2017
By Mills & Boon, an imprint of HarperCollins*Publishers*
1 London Bridge Street, London, SE1 9GF

ISBN: 978-0-263-93330-7

Printed and bound in Spain
by CPI, Barcelona